I0720536

MYSTERY ON THE ARGYLE PLAINS

Book 4 in the Series

The Trail of Blood and Wine

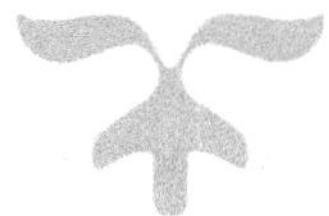

PAUL AND MERRILL BONARRIGO

Mystery on the Argyle Plains

Book Four in the Series

Trails of Blood and Wine

Copyright © 2024 Merbon
All Rights Reserved

No part of this book may be used or reproduced in any manner whatsoever without written permission, except in the case of brief quotations embodied in critical articles and reviews. For reprint permission, please contact the publisher.

This book is a work of fiction. The acknowledged historical background for this work of fiction has been represented accurately to the best of the authors' ability, regarding events, places, and people.

The incidents in the book are not intended to be true depictions of actual events. There are historical characters and fictional characters woven into the story. The real characters are important individuals in Texas wine history. Any resemblance to actual persons by the fictional characters, places, or events is entirely coincidental.

Publisher: Merbon
4401 Old Reliance Road
Bryan, Texas 77808
979-820-1238

Mer-bon.com/story/

@mer-bon

Copyeditor and Cover Design: Abby Parker

Soft Cover ISBN: 978-1-7361770-7-5

eBook ISBN: 978-1-7361770-8-2

To Paul and Karen Bonarrigo,

To our grandchildren Paul Anthony and

Sophia Marie Bonarrigo,

the next generation of Texas wine pioneers,

and

To the Lord who has so blessed us.

May the Lord forever bless you and guide your paths.

"I am the vine; you are the branches. If you remain in me and I in you, you will bear much fruit; apart from me you can do nothing."

John 15:5

The Trail of Blood and Wine
Mystery on the Argyle Plains

Chapter 1

Hi, I am Trevor Talan, assistant professor at Texas A&M University in Bryan-College Station, Texas. I grew up in Oklahoma in a career military family and love viticulture, enology, and the pursuit of intrigue. You may have heard about my ability to investigate and solve murders involving the Texas wine industry.

I am a graduate of State University and have been fortunate to receive an appointment at Texas A&M University when the grandfather of the Texas wine industry, Dr. George Ray McEachern, retired.

I helped solve the **"Curse of Estacado"** - my first murder mystery involvement. Then I assisted in solving the mystery of **"Blood on the Brazos"**. Most recently I helped solve **"Death on the Pedernales"**.

I had just come back from Christmas vacation in Oklahoma when I received a call from the Arrgos family in North Texas.

"Hello, Trevor, this is Oto Arrgos. My wife Bea and I were introduced to you by the President of the Texas Wine & Growers Association at the

North Texas conference. I am calling to get your help in our vineyard and to see if you know a good winemaker consultant to help us with improving our wine quality."

It was a delight to hear from him. The Arrgos family is a well-established North Texas winery with a wonderful reputation within the industry.

Oto is a six-generation Albanian who came to America to practice medicine but was unable to secure a medical license due to his medical school not being approved by the American Medical Association. Since he had a strong background in chemistry and a family upbringing in wine, he chose to open a winery in Texas.

He and his wife Bea pioneered grape growing in North Texas. Oto is up in years and is rumored to be ready to retire.

They had told me it was their secret hope that their daughter Kristy, a petit dark-haired woman, would someday take over the winery even though she showed no interest growing up and chose to teach instead.

Oto chuckled, "She was and is my delight. As our only child, she received all of our love, attention, and encouragement. With that also came great expectations.

"She attended SMU majoring in math and became a high school level math teacher. As an average student herself, she had empathy for her own students who needed more help to understand the material.

"Travel was her passion. Each summer she traveled to Europe for summer classes in art and music. Though ambitious for her own dreams, she was always respectful of us. I look forward to you meeting her. Here is her phone number so you can connect with her about the vineyard."

"Oto," I said, "it is wonderful to hear from you and I am happy to help. My winemaker consultant friend is Philip Moore who lives in Grapevine, Texas, and has helped many wineries. I will reach out to him. Do you mind if I bring my girlfriend Lulu? You met her at the North Texas conference."

Oto responded, "We would love to have her. I think our daughter, Kristy, will love her. Lulu never seems to meet a stranger and has a kind face and warm heart. Bea and I were very impressed when we first met her. She came up to me and Bea and gave us warm hugs like we had been friends forever. She even greeted us with an Albanian greeting, 'Tungjatjeta', which is our way of greeting a friend in Albania. Bea said, as soon as she met Lulu, 'She is a keeper.'"

During the conference where I met the Arrgos', Oto and Bea shared their history. Oto told me that he grew up in a small Albanian city, Ksamil, which is considered one of the most beautiful cities in Albania. Founded on the crystal-clear waters of the Ionian Sea, it has a stunning mountain backdrop.

Oto attended the University of Medicine in Tirana, Albania, following in the footsteps of his father who was a well-respected surgeon. He was the first cardiovascular surgeon to perform a heart transplant in Albania. Oto told me that he felt he had big shoes to fill there.

Bea shared, "Oto was a star soccer player. As Center Striker he held the record for most goals scored in a single game. In his playing days he stood six feet two inches tall and was a lean 180 pounds. He was the fastest man on the field."

The legend is that on corner kicks he could jump more than a foot higher than any other player, and he even played on the Albanian junior Olympic team. He was a strong burly man with an athletic build and had a handshake that you would never forget. His grip was like putting your hand in a vice and his skin resembled a lumberjack from years in the sun as a vinetender.

Bea continued, "We met in high school. Oto was the captain on the soccer team and I was the president of the student body. We traveled in different circles in high school and never dated but I always admired him. I came from a family of humble means."

Bea is very modest. Oto had shared with me that she was the prettiest girl in her high school.

"Her hair flowed down to her waste," he reminisced. "She was very popular but her schoolwork was always a priority. She received a full academic scholarship to attend the college of her choice."

I could tell he was very proud for her.

"Her dad was a fisherman," added Oto. "And Bea helped the family with paying bills and keeping books. She followed me to the university in Tirana and studied at the business college there."

Bea told me a story once about how she really fell in love with Oto.

"One beautiful Albanian day Oto asked me to go out on a boat. How very romantic, I thought, even though I was nervous since I could not swim.

"There was a cool breeze and the sun shone brightly. Oto was telling me his favorite soccer stories. I was laughing as he made grandiose gestures with his arms demonstrating a soccer goalie save when suddenly a big wave capsized the boat.

"Oto grabbed my arm with one hand and quickly righted the boat with the other. Then he lifted me out of the water back into the boat. He was so strong!

"Then he struggled to get himself into the boat but kept falling back into the water. The waves were high and his arms were tired. Without thinking, I immediately reached my hand out to Oto and, with what must have been superhuman strength, lifted him into the boat. God must have been with me. My heart was pounding.

"As we paused to catch our breath, we watched the oars of the boat float away. Oto tried to move the boat with his hands. It went nowhere. Looking at each other we began to laugh. We were dripping wet and I had seaweed hanging over my shoulder.

"All we could do was just sit there in the boat, stranded. An hour later my father came by in his fishing boat to tow us back into the port.

"While we were stranded we talked, laughed, and talked. It felt like we had known each other all of our lives. It became crystal clear to me that Oto was my soulmate and my hero. He saved my life and I saved Oto's life."

Bea, a petit, blond-haired and hazel-eyed beauty, always appeared to be cheerful and looked upon life in a positive way.

"My father did not like Oto at first. Oto was from an aristocratic family and my father was afraid that Oto would grow tired of my humble upbringing. Oto proved him wrong," she smiled, "Oto told my father that I had a warm and sincere heart."

Oto chipped in, "Bea's optimistic opinion about the earth and all the people she knows is refreshing. I told her father that he had raised the most wonderful person inside and out."

Bea smiled and said, "That compliment changed my father's heart about Oto. From that day forward Oto could do no wrong in my father's eyes."

After graduating from college and medical school, Oto and Bea married. It did not take long for them to realize that there was little opportunity in Albania.

In Albania, doctors worked for the government and were paid slightly more than schoolteachers. The opportunity for private practice was nearly impossible.

With a leap of faith and no money in their pockets, they hitched a ride on an Albanian cargo ship that was headed to America. Both of them worked in the galley to pay for their board.

I asked them about that experience and Oto replied, "We lived among the crew, worked sixteen hours per day, and the trip took two weeks. Despite working in the kitchen, we both lost ten pounds."

They laughed and shared that they had been overjoyed to finally arrive in the United States of America.

Bea reminisced, "We arrived at the Port of Galveston penniless, unable to speak good English, and clueless about where in the world Galveston, Texas was. Friendly Texans helped us find a place to stay and gave us contacts for jobs. Oto immediately enlisted into the United States military, and I got a job in a restaurant.

"Oto served in the navy as a corpsman. He served aboard "The Mercy", the navy's hospital ship. Ironically, he spent two years assisting earthquake victims in Italy, Albania, and Croatia.

"After his military service, Oto joined me to work in that same restaurant. The owner made us feel like family. He had no children or heirs. We so appreciated his kindness in helping us to adapt to our new American life. When the owner died he gave Oto and me the restaurant. We built the business, sold the restaurant to the Landry restaurant group, and used the money to start the winery."

Bea's and Oto's hard work allowed them the opportunity to pay to have their parents immigrate to America. Living out their lives in Argyle in small homes that Oto and Bea were able to purchase for them, they enjoyed seeing their children's successes in living the American dream.

Their story enamored me and Lulu. Family is everything. Lulu lost her biological family and came to Texas as an orphan. She really appreciates family.

Family is why Oto and Bea worked so hard to be successful and why they stayed so involved in the Texas wine industry.

 After hearing the struggles of Oto and Bea in coming to America and knowing Lulu grew up in an orphanage, I thought back on how blessed I was. My dad was gone serving our country in the military but he made up for it when he came home.

My mom always made herself available to me. My family did not have to immigrate. Thank the Lord that I have a family that supported me and shaped my life.

Chapter 2

"Trevor, please tell me about Philip Moore," inquired Oto.

"Philip is a native Californian from the bay area who went to school at Fresno State. He interned at Gallo and after graduation worked at Gallo Sonoma. After working at Gallo for ten years he moved to Australia and worked for Red Tail Winery.

"At Red Tail, Philip became frustrated with many of his workers. They seemed to enjoy themselves too much on the weekends and would often not show up to work on Mondays or would come to work hungover.

"On one occasion a worker did not connect a hose to a 50,000-gallon tank before opening the valve. Thousands of gallons of wine poured onto the floor. Philip heard the noise, walked into the tank room, and saw his worker trying to stop the flow of the wine out of the tank with his hands while calling for help. Just imagine the pressure of 50,000 gallons of wine flowing out of a tank. With both hands trying to hold back the flow he could not.

"Philip ran to the tank and stopped the tragedy by merely shutting the valve. Realizing that he needed to practice his winemaking skills elsewhere, he returned to the United States.

"Since Texas is the fastest growing wine industry in the United States, he decided to settle in Grapevine, Texas. His wife works for P W McCallum, the Director of the Grapevine Visitor and Convention Bureau.

"PW was at the North Texas Grape Growers meeting as well. Bea met him. She told me that PW is one of the most respected Visitor and Convention Bureau directors in the United States.

"Philip has a lot of experience and is a good family man. You will enjoy collaborating with him."

Oto asked, "That sounds good, Trevor, when can you come to the vineyard?"

"It looks like I can come up January 14th." I replied, "My teaching duties at Texas A&M have not begun. Lulu and I are both free. How are you and Bea?"

Oto was exuberant, "Life is good! Bea's health is fantastic. We are excited that our daughter Kristy will be taking over the winery."

I was surprised, "I thought Kristy is an educator and has no experience in the wine industry."

"It is amazing how things can change, Trevor. Kristy was teaching in an inner-city high school in New York," shared Oto. "She was teaching at Roosevelt High School in the Bronx and loved her students. Kristy rented an apartment on Arthur Avenue, the center of Italian/American culture in

New York. She loved shopping at the Mayor LaGuardia retail market and learned to cook authentic Italian foods with fresh meat, produce, cheese and pastries.

"Her favorite restaurant was Mario's. She loved their Osso Buco which is veal shank braised to render meat so tender it falls off the bone.

"Roosevelt high school was a seven-block walk. It is directly across from Fordham University. In the last two years the influx of illegal aliens has dramatically changed the neighborhood.

"She was assaulted by an illegal alien from Venezuela. He approached her and called her a white woman who hated people from Venezuela. Kristy recognized her assailant as one of her students that she had failed for not turning in any homework. She spent two days in Fordham hospital. Her assailant turned out to be a repeat offender and all he received was probation. Can you imagine?

"Half of the high school was converted to housing for the immigrants. To make up for losing half of the classroom space, Kristy had to teach from 7:00 am to 1:00 pm for the first student group and then from 1:30 pm to 6:30 pm for the second group. She was exhausted and fearful for her safety. We were fearful for her.

"In the wintertime it gets dark at 5:00 pm. Getting out at 6:30 pm means she was walking home in the dark, which was too dangerous. She hated to leave her students but was happy to say goodbye to the Bronx.

"At the end of the fall semester in New York, Kristy gave notice and she called me to say she was ready to come back to the family winery. I said, 'Praise the Lord!'

"That is why we need a consultant, Trevor.

"It is very difficult for the older generation to train the younger generation. They are often not receptive and they think our methods are antiquated. Bea and I are preparing to retire, and we need to make sure that everything is in place to help with a successful transition."

"I understand," I said, "and look forward to seeing you. It is a blessing that you and Bea can retire and know that the winery is in family hands. The Texas wine industry has several families in transition to the next generation now.

"Did you hear that Burning Bush's owners Mabel and Marcom sold their winery to their grandchildren, Lyndon and Laura? They were working in the Peace Corp in Ethiopia and developed a love of Italian varietals. You know, Ethiopia had a lot of Italians settle and start wineries there."

Oto said, "I have not met them yet. I like Italian varietals and believe there is tremendous potential for them in Texas. Texans are not very familiar with the Italian varieties. In Italy they usually label the wine based on location instead of variety. Our baby boomer customers who know the wines by location are dying off and drinking less. We need Arrgos Cellars to appeal to younger customers familiar with varietal wines. Kristy is young and will bring new ideas to a well-established winery.

"On top of that, Héctor, our vineyard manager of many years, threatened to retire and is very set in his ways."

I said, "Oto, tell me more about Héctor."

"Héctor is from Baja, California, and worked in the grape industry there. He was raised by his grandmother. His father was abusive and was put in prison for almost killing his mother. He spent five years in a Mexican prison. After his father was released, he abandoned his family. His mother passed away when Hector was only twelve years old.

"Hector was educated through the eighth grade then went to work in the Baja Vineyards. He worked his way up to vineyard manager at Casa Filecio in Baja. That is where Bea and I met him on a vacation to that region. I was curious about the vineyard and found Hector working in the vineyard. He seemed very knowledgeable and I told him if he ever came to the USA to reach out to me.

"Soon after that he obtained a work visa to work for me as a vineyard worker. Eventually, he earned my trust to be the vineyard manager.

"Hector met his wife locally at a dance. Hector was a good dancer and his wife Stella was very impressed with his moves. He told me she asked him to dance and even cut in on a dance he was having with another woman. That was how they met. As long as they were on the dance floor, they seemed ok.

"Then after marriage Hector was not as eager to dance all the time. He was tired at night and wanted to relax. Stella got bored.

"Their marriage has been a rocky one. Both of them are very hot-tempered.

He is self-taught and is very dedicated. The problem is that he is very impulsive and has run off many vineyard workers. We even had a complaint filed on us with the employment commission. One time, a vineyard worker drove the tractor over an end post and I thought Héctor was going to beat him to a pulp."

I responded with a bit of alarm, "Is he dangerous? Should I be concerned?"

Oto reassured me, "I sent him to an anger management program and he has been fine ever since. You will have to win him over and introduce new ideas gradually.

"The other problem is that Héctor's wife, Stella, has also been giving Héctor grief. She recently retired from her job and has been threatening to leave Héctor.

"When he said he would retire, I had mixed emotions. I feared that his absence would result in additional vineyard work that would be an added burden to Kristy, but I was relieved to know that if he were gone, the drama would go with him.

"He does have an assistant manager, José, who worked for Casa Madeira, in Parras, Mexico. It is the oldest winery in the Americas. Other than that, I do not know very much about him."

I reassured Oto, "If Kristy can handle teaching in the Bronx, New York, she can certainly run such a wonderful winery. You and Bea have laid a strong foundation. Does she have other support?"

"Yes she does, Trevor. Kristy met a wonderful young man who is an attorney in Dallas. His name is Mathew Koreni. This is the first time I have seen Kristy so taken by a young man. Mathew is respectful of her and she loves him."

"Thank you for calling, Oto," and thank you for your confidence in me. I look forward to seeing you on the 14th."

When I got home, I explained to Lulu where I was going and asked her if she wanted to come with me.

"Trevor," she giggled, "You know I love traveling with you! Driving from College Station to Dallas will be fun. I have never been to Argyle but did hear that it is a lovely town in Denton County with many horse farms."

Lulu was so excited about the trip to Argyle that she showed me the route she wanted us to take without going on the interstate. Her route would take us through Mexia, Fairfield, Waxahachie, Dallas, Grapevine, and finally to Argyle.

I told her, "You know, this sounds interesting since many of these towns I have never seen, but it adds about one and a half hours more to the trip."

She replied, "I love January. The trees are bare and there is a peaceful quiet to the landscape. You can see the rolling hills. Most people prefer spring but winter is my favorite time of year.

"Plus, did you know that Argyle is famous for great BBQ restaurants? We could go to 407 BBQ or Bumbashed BBQ. I love BBQ!

"When I was a teenager, we had BBQ every weekend at the orphanage. I would help add wood to the fire and brush the BBQ sauce on the meat. The smell of the pit made my mouth water."

"I learn new things about you every day, Lulu."

Chapter 3

On the morning of January 14th, Lulu and I drove from College Station to Argyle. On the way she insisted we stop at Sam's Original Restaurant in Fairfield, Texas. There we got a romantic booth in the corner. Lulu always prefers a booth in the corner. I like them because there is more room and I can easily observe everything going on around us.

Our waitress, Matilda, told us in a rich southern accent, "The feature of the day is a chicken fried steak smothered in honey cream sauce. And today's featured pie is Key Lime."

It is a good thing we decided to share the chicken fried steak because it was the biggest chicken fried steak we had ever seen. It covered the entire plate and was smothered in mouthwatering white gravy.

Lulu also wanted us to stop at Jimmy's Food Store in Dallas. They have everything Italian! Lulu encouraged me to buy their muffaletta. She knows I love muffalettas. We got it to go because I was already full of the chicken fried steak.

My first encounter with this amazing sandwich was in New Orleans at the restaurant I love the most, Cochon Butcher. I tried to recreate the recipe.

Trevor's Muffaletta Recipe

Ingredients

For the Olive Salad

- *1 cup green olives, pitted and chopped*
- *1 cup black olives, pitted and chopped*
- *½ cup roasted red peppers, chopped*
- *¼ cup celery, finely chopped*
- *¼ cup carrots, finely chopped*
- *¼ pepperoncini, chopped*
- *¼ cup capers, drained*
- *¼ cup flat-leaf parsley, chopped*
- *3 cloves garlic, minced*
- *½ cup olive oil*
- *¼ cup red wine vinegar*
- *¼ cup Messina Hof Angel Late Harvest Riesling*
- *1 teaspoon dried oregano*
- *1 teaspoon dried basil*
- *Salt and pepper to taste*

For the sandwich

- *1 large round loaf of Italian bread*
- *¼ pound soppressata, thinly sliced*
- *¼ pound ham, thinly sliced*
- *¼ pound salami, thinly sliced*
- *¼ pound provolone cheese, thinly sliced*
- *¼ pound mozzarella cheese, thinly sliced*

Preparation

1. *In a large bowl, combine the green olives, black olives, roasted red peppers, celery, carrots, pepperoncini, capers, parsley, and garlic.*

2. *In a separate bowl, whisk together the olive oil, red wine vinegar, Angel wine, oregano, basil, salt, and pepper.*

3. *Pour the dressing over the olive mixture and toss to combine.*

4. *Cover and refrigerate for at least one hour, preferably overnight, to allow the flavors to meld.*

5. *Cut the round loaf of Italian bread in half horizontally. Hollow out some of the bread from the top and bottom halves to make room for the filling.*

6. *Spread a generous amount of the olive salad evenly over the cut sides of both halves of the bread.*

7. *Layer the soppressata, ham, salami, provolone cheese, and mozzarella cheese on the bottom half of the bread.*

8. *Place the top half of the bread over the layered ingredients to form a sandwich.*

9. *Wrap the sandwich tightly in plastic wrap. Place a heavy object (like a cast-iron skillet) on top of the wrapped sandwich and let it press for at least 30 minutes.*

10. *Unwrap the sandwich and cut it into serving portions.*

Lulu knows her food. You would never know how much she enjoys eating. She looks very athletic.

As we came into Argyle, I stopped by the sheriff's department on the way to the Arrgos vineyard in order to introduce myself. It is a standard procedure for me in every town where I work. Lulu and I went inside.

The station looked like a throwback of the Wild West. There were animal heads adorning the walls and a sheriff came through swinging saloon style doors to greet us. It was just like being on a movie set. He was tall, bowlegged, and slim with a handlebar mustache. He wore Lucchese cowboy boots and a white cowboy hat.

"What can we do for you?" he asked slowly in a deep Texas drawl.

"My name is Trevor Talan and this is my girlfriend Lulu. We are headed to the Arrgos vineyard. I am a viticulturist and investigator and may be in this area for a few days. Here is my contact information in case you or anyone needs horticulture assistance."

"Welcome to Argyle, my name is Sheriff Longo. What is a viticulturalist and what kind of investigator are you?"

Appreciative that he showed an interest I said, "A viticulturalist is a person who works with vineyards. I went to school at State University but am now with the extension service at Texas A&M University.

"As a consultant to the grape industry in Texas, I have to investigate problems associated with the vineyard and provide solutions. I have worked extensively in West Texas vineyards, East Texas vineyards, Hill Country vineyards, and now North Texas vineyards. I will be consulting with the Arrgos family."

"Your timing is uncanny," said Sheriff Longo, "I know the Arrgos family well. I am godfather to their daughter Kristy and have known Oto and Bea ever since they came to town.

"We just received an urgent dispatch to Arrgos Cellars. That is very unusual because if it had been a routine request then Oto would have called me directly. I do know that he was going to Grapevine for the weekend to give a presentation for the Texas Wine and Grape Growers Association meeting.

"I do not know what the problem is, but you are welcome to come along since you are going that way anyway."

I asked the sheriff how far it is to the winery. He replied, "This is a small town so nothing is very far away. It is a pretty drive through horse farms and pecan orchards."

Lulu clapped enthusiastically. Sheriff Longo looked at her incredulously over his glasses. She smiled and explained her love of horses. He nodded and smiled.

The winding road to Arrgos Winery provided visual surprises of beautiful farms, Kelly green pastures, and impressive homes. As we drove, we could see horses running playfully in the pastures. There were horse farms after horse farms. Lulu loves horses.

She reminisced, "The orphanage in the Brazos Bottom where I grew up had quarter and cutting horses. My chore was to clean the stables and brush the horses. I learned to ride by the time I was ten years old."

She often told me how she could communicate with her horses. Seeing these horses brought back tender memories for her.

The oak and pecan trees had shed their leaves but the pine trees filled the landscape with brilliant green colors. The clouds were large and puffy. Lulu described all the shapes she was seeing as we drove. One of the things we love to do is lie in our yard, look at the stars at night and watch the cloud shapes during the day.

Chapter 4

It was a cold, dark day in January. The vineyard was bleak.

Lulu loved it. "Listen to the wind howling," she mused."

The vines were dormant. Not one green leaf was in sight. There was an eeriness. A group of vultures circled in the sky eyeing a dead object below. Suddenly, a man stepped out in front of our car. Brakes grinded. Lulu squealed.

Sheriff Longo shook his head and waved, "It is the vineyard manager, Héctor, making his daily rounds of the vineyard. He has worked here as manager since the winery began twenty years ago. Now he says he is about to retire.

"When I asked Héctor why he was retiring, he mentioned that all of his recent requests for new equipment were rejected by Oto and Bea because the winery is having financial troubles."

I nodded, "That is why I am here to help Oto and Héctor with the vineyard."

Sheriff Longo stopped the car to speak to Héctor. It was Monday.

"Hello, Héctor. What is going on here?"

Héctor reported, "I drove through the vineyard, noticing that vultures were landing. When I got close, I was shocked to see that there was a body lying in the mud. That is when I called the Sheriff's department."

"Héctor, how did you find the body?" Sheriff asked.

Héctor pointed in the direction of the vultures. "I was making my daily rounds, noticed the vultures landing, and drove to the spot. When I got there, they were ripping apart a body. The face of the body was completely chewed and unidentifiable.

"People normally walk through the vineyard but not in January. I have not seen anyone other than my staff in the vineyard for weeks. Sheriff Longo, who do you think the body is?"

Sheriff replied, "I do not know but I called our forensic group to start the investigation.

"Héctor, this is Trevor Talan. He is a viticulturist and investigator who has come to us from Texas A&M University."

Héctor looked at me and grumbled, "So you're the vineyard consultant that Oto told me he had contacted to increase the yield and quality of the vineyard."

Héctor's face looked stone cold and his black eyes glared at me.

I extended my hand to shake and told him that I looked forward to working with him. Hector just smirked and walked away.

As we walked away from Héctor, Sheriff Longo told me, "You will have your hands full with Héctor. He has been in charge for twenty years and has had run of the place.

"He has his hands full with his wife. I know his wife. She recently retired from the Argyle Inn. When she ran the front desk and managed the bar, I had to break up many fights. She is a real flirt and seems to encourage jealous confrontations to inspire more tips. It is good for the Inn that she retired. There should be less fights to break up."

He laughed, "They hired a retired Episcopal priest to replace her. Since he has been there he has already changed the names of some of the drinks. They now serve John the Baptist margaritas and their wine list is called the Feast of Cana Selections. Their business has really picked up. All of the Episcopal, Lutheran, and Catholics now flock to the bar.

"Where will you be staying?"

I explained that Oto had invited us to stay at the guest house.

"It is great that you can help Kristy in her transition to ownership," said Sheriff, "I am pleased that she will have your guidance. There are many changes happening in her life. I am also thankful that she has Mathew Koreni.

"I was at the engagement party and could feel their love and respect for one another."

I asked Sheriff how they met.

"Kristy told us they met when she was vacationing in Port Aransas. When dining at the Seafood and Spaghetti Warehouse, Kristy said she was approached by a *'handsome tanned-skin man with big brown cow eyes and impeccable manners'*.

"Due to his tan, she thought he was from Corpus Christi but was pleased to find out that he was from Dallas. He explained that he got his tan because he likes to play golf.

"He impressed her by buying a glass of Messina Hof Pinot Grigio and personally delivering it to her table. It was love at first sip. I cannot tell you how good it is to have her home.

"When I heard she had taken a teaching job in New York, I feared for her. Once I went to New York and took my wife to Central Park. Before I knew it there was a group of youth harassing us. I have no fond memories of New York."

Lulu chirped in, "I have never been to New York. There are so many reports of violence there. But, now here in Texas, I see a dead body in a vineyard. Please excuse me, I need to go to the tasting room."

Hector volunteered to take her. On the way he told Lulu that he did not understand why Oto called Trevor to consult. "I believe that I could work with Kristy and improve the vineyard."

Lulu reassured Hector, "Trevor is easy to work with."

Concerned about the direction of the conversation, Lulu was happy when they pulled up to the retail room and she was able to get out.

Chapter 5

"Trevor, lets carefully examine the scene," said Sheriff Longo as he turned his attention to the crime at hand. "We have not had a suspicious death in Argyle for more than ten years."

He looked around and observed, "It is good that it had been raining. The vineyard land holds water, so we should be able to see footprints and any vehicle tracks."

There were tire tracks leading up to the body and ditches surrounding the body. The sheriff shared that the tire tracks looked like a 4-wheeler due to the narrow wheelbase, and that he knew the winery owned one. It was the one Héctor used to make rounds of the vineyard.

We walked back to Héctor who said, "I noticed something strange when I started the 4-wheeler. The key was left in the ignition. I normally store the key in the glove compartment. It must have been someone else who was driving the 4-wheeler."

I asked, "Who all had access to the 4-wheeler key?"

Héctor responded, "At least six people have access to it."

The coroner and Sheriff's team arrived quickly, cordoned off the property and began investigating. I stayed to help them while Sheriff

Longo helped the coroner transport the body to Argyle Morgue.

Twenty feet from where the body had laid, I found the trunk of a dead grapevine stained with blood. The team took fingerprints and DNA samples from the grapevine trunk. The bark of the trunk was very irregular and obviously from a very old plant because the trunk had a wide girth. I suspected the blood would probably be from the victim.

The back wheels of the 4-wheeler made deep mud tracks as though the vehicle was stuck. One of the sheriff's team told me that it had rained all last week and that the vineyard received six inches of rain.

The 4-wheeler must have been in 2-wheel drive because it looked like the killer had to drive the 4-wheeler back and forth, back and forth, back and forth, over the body in order to avoid getting stuck. When we checked the winery 4-wheeler, it was still left in 2-wheel drive.

The team took soil samples and impressions of the tire tracks. As I surveyed the area, I saw footprints of a medium-sized person. The team took impressions of the footprints as well.

The ground was very disturbed near the tire tracks so it looked as though there was a struggle. The footprints that were found appeared to be of two people. One person had street shoes and the other had work shoes suitable for the outdoors.

Two grapevines were knocked down which must have been caused by the 4-wheeler backing up. The clear identifiable tracks of the 4-wheeler were headed toward the winery as it left the crime scene.

Everyone followed me to the 4-wheeler, which was parked outside of the retail shop. The back tires were covered in mud. The back bumper looked as though it had run into something. There was damage to the undercarriage. The sheriff's team took fingerprints and DNA off of the key and left.

Sheriff Longo went to speak to the coroner and said he would call me when he knew more.

I grabbed a ride with Sheriff back to the office to get my car. That glass of Pinot Grigio sounded really good so I joined Lulu in the tasting room and left money on the counter for a bottle of Pinot Grigio before we headed to the guest house.

That night in the guest house Lulu told me that Kristy had told the retail manager that she was fearful about her future role at the winery.

"According to the manager, Kristy said that Oto was constantly under verbal attack by people who were jealous of the winery's successes. She admired how strong and diplomatic he was and expressed concern that she could not be so strong."

I asked her what type of verbal attacks.

Lulu said, "There was someone that called and left negative messages about Oto's wine and posted lies about the source of his grapes.

"The retail manager also shared that she got a call from a friend who was attending the Texas Wine and Grape Grower meeting in Grapevine. The friend asked why Oto did not show up for his panel presentation."

Lulu was not the type of person to just drop a strong concern. She immediately got on her phone and checked Arrgos Cellars social media, "Most of the comments are wonderful but there are two hateful comments about Oto and where he sourced his grapes."

She showed me one from an account named "Hill Country Truth" who appeared to be a male.

"The posts claim that Oto bought wine from California," Lulu stated, "So, I went and looked at all the labels in the retail room. They all say, 'Made from 100% Texas Grapes'.

"The second post claimed the Arrgos wines are produced and bottled in California but lists a Texas location," she added.

"I hope Kristy does not get too discouraged," she continued. "I have not even met her yet but feel her anxiety."

I hugged Lulu. "Lulu, you are always so sensitive to other people's feelings. It is something I love about you but please forget about Kristy's concerns. Enjoy the beauty of this guest house, the peace of the vineyard, and our time together."

Chapter 6

The next day the coroner announced the news to Sheriff Longo and me, "The dead body is that of Oto Arrgos. He was run over by a 4-wheeler and his head was traumatized.

"He did not die immediately. He probably died hours after being run over. If it had been an accident, the person who ran him over him could have gotten help for Oto. This was not an accident. It appears to be murder."

The sheriff thanked the coroner for such a quick result.

Then the coroner said, "Sheriff, there was much more. During my coronary autopsy, I found that Oto had advanced pancreatic cancer with probably only a few months to live.

"When I called his daughter Kristy to inform her that her father was dead and ask about Oto's cancer, she was shocked. There was a long moment of silence. I could hear Kristy's staccato breathing as she fought back tears. When she got back on the phone her voice was muffled and interrupted by tears. She was obviously shocked.

"She asked me what happened. She said that she was in California attending a wine education program and did not know anything about the death. I told her that we were investigating the death and that we could tell her more when she got home."

The Coroner said, "Then I shared that during the autopsy of her father's body I found pancreatic cancer. I asked her if she knew about the cancer.

"There was a pause as if she were collecting her thoughts and then replied, *'Oto was a very private person. He never said a word about it. He never told me about any of his doctor visits.'* Kristy was crying. Then she added, *'I will have to ask my mother what she knows about it.'* Then she thanked me for the call and quickly got off the phone. It was obvious she was devastated."

Sheriff Longo looked at me and said, "That is really unusual. Kristy and her dad were very close. They normally shared everything. As Oto and Bea's only child, Oto thought Kristy hung the moon. Oto was a bigger than life person. That must have been so hard for Kristy to process that her father was dead."

Sheriff Longo then decided to call Danny, the winery's attorney and good friend of Oto, Bea and Kristy. He is also the District Attorney.

"Danny, this is Sheriff Longo. I wanted personally to let you know that our dear friend, Oto, is dead and it appears that he was murdered."

I could not hear the other end of the conversation, but I saw Sheriff's eyes tear up and could tell that

Danny must have been emotional on the other end of the phone call. Sheriff did say, "There are many suspects but no conclusion."

So, I could only guess that Danny asked if we knew who the murderer was. The conversation was short and Sheriff Longo wiped his eyes on his sleeve after hanging up.

Sheriff looked at me, "I wonder if Bea knew about the cancer. I did not even know about the cancer. Oto and I were close friends."

Sheriff and I went to Héctor and asked, "Where is Bea? Can we talk with her?"

Héctor did not respond.

Sheriff asked, "Héctor, where can we find Bea?"

Héctor looked away and asked if we had checked with her at home. "I know she managed retail all weekend," he added. "She is probably tired."

On the way to Bea's house, I told the Sheriff, "It really gave me a new perspective on why Oto had such a sense of urgency to transfer ownership of the winery and vineyard to Kristy and why he wanted me to come and bring a wine consultant."

Bea's home was locked up and dark. We checked the back door and all around the house. Everything was locked up and Bea's car was not in the garage or in the driveway.

I asked Sheriff Longo, "You mentioned that you were close to Oto but how well did you know Oto and Bea?"

Sheriff Longo replied, "I have known them ever since they opened the winery. When I ran for Sheriff they did fundraisers at the winery for me.

"When Kristy was born they asked me to be the Godfather. Oto and Bea were active in their church, supported many charities, and provided internships to students from the local junior college.

"They were devoted to each other and did everything together. It seems very strange that Bea is not at home."

There was a pause while the sheriff was thinking. I remained quiet out of respect.

"Trevor, now that I think of it, there was one intern just two months ago that Oto had to dismiss."

"Why did he have to be dismissed?" I asked.

"Oto caught him stealing bags of fertilizer." Said Sheriff, "I'll have to look up my police reports for the details. When the intern was dismissed, he got so violent that Oto called me to escort the intern off the winery property.

"Because of the police report and failed internship, he could not graduate with his class. A month later Oto found two of his tractor tires slit with a sharp blade. Revenge could have been the motive.

"The tire incidents are still unsolved, Trevor. The intern moved away and my office has been unable to find him."

I asked Sheriff if he heard about the two social media posts Lulu had found. He had not so I showed him some photos associated in the profile page of Hill Country Truth.

Sheriff looked carefully and pointed to one saying, "That was the intern."

Chapter 7

Sheriff Longo called Kristy. She explained that she was at a short course in winemaking and vineyard management at University of California at Davis. She expressed appreciation that Bea was managing the winery while Kristy was gone.

She told Sheriff, "When I got the call from the coroner, I was devastated. My exuberant joy of achieving my winemaking certificate was replaced with tears of anguish and grief. I knew that dad would be so proud of me for getting my certificate. I was excited to share it with him.

"Then in a blink of an eye he was gone. I cannot share with him the fulfillment of his dream for me. He was my protector, my rock, my life teacher." She broke into tears.

"I am sorry, Sheriff," she apologized, "He was your friend. I know you feel the loss, too."

She jumped on the next plane and flew home. Sheriff Longo and I met her at the airport Tuesday evening.

As Kristy got off the plane, Sheriff Longo gave her a big hug and told her how sorry he was for her loss. "Oto was a good friend," he said, "I will miss him dearly."

Sheriff introduced us. Kristy was gracious. Despite her grief she reached out and gave me a hug.

It struck me how fragile life is and how important close relationships are to each of us. Another day on this earth is never guaranteed. I am reminded how important it is to tell those individuals close to us how much we love them each day.

On the way back to the winery, I asked Kristy when she last spoke with her father, Oto.

"I spoke with him Friday morning before my classes started," she replied. "He told me about you and a wine consultant coming to the vineyard. It seemed that he was so much more at peace knowing that he had a plan.

"Dad always planned ahead." She paused, "Mom told me that even on the day of their wedding he showed up two hours before the ceremony was to start.

"In the early days of the winery Dad worked in the vineyard every day, did his own labs, and wrote orders to make the wine. He worked very hard to make good wines that would bring honor to Texas.

"He promised me the wine consultant would collaborate with me to make my first vintage. He wanted me to be able to carry on the family wine legacy. He and I were very excited about it. Dad always planned ahead. He thought of everything."

Kristy said, "Everyone loved my dad. He and my mother were pioneers in the North Texas wine industry. Mom was the M.O.M. of the winery."

I was curious and asked, "What does M.O.M. stand for?"

Kristy replied, "MOM stands for Mentor. Organizer. Motivator. She even has that on her nametag.

"Mom developed each department of the winery as they grew and then hired a manager to run that area. That made her the perfect person to train the new hires.

"Helping our employees, caring for the guests, keeping the place organized, and running the winery was natural for her. She was the perfect business partner for Dad.

"She also offers John 15 tours of the vineyard. It is her calling. Churches from all around book John 15 tours so Bea can explain the significance of the Bible verse on our daily lives.

"Dad was really the heart of the winery and mom is the soul of the winery."

I asked Kristy, "Why did Oto serve in the navy when there was no draft?"

Kristy answered, "My dad arrived in the USA illegally from Albania and his path to citizenship was by serving in the military.

"In August of 1990, the Gulf war had just begun. Oto was afraid of deportation, so he enlisted in the navy as a medic.

"Dad attended medical school in Albania but was not eligible to be a physician in the United States. After serving two years aboard "The Mercy" hospital ship, he was eligible for US citizenship. Then, my mother obtained her citizenship through my dad.

"Mom told me that she was so smitten with Oto but she did not think he noticed her except as a friend, like a little sister. Then he began to walk her to classes, wait for her in the hallways, carry her books, and even asked to sit with her at lunch. That was a huge deal because other boys would make fun of him, but he just smiled and said they were jealous.

"They always told me that the Lord has a plan and that He works all things together for good. Their lives certainly spoke to that.

"Mom was a Certified Public Accountant in Albania, so she was the perfect person to run the winery. Dad was the perfect winemaker. His chemistry background from medical school and amazing nose gave him the tools needed to make great wines. Blending is the secret of great wines and he could take average grapes and turn them into medal winning wines.

"Mom loved to cook. Food and wine pairing became her passion. She was able to take dad's great wines and make them sing by pairing the perfect foods with them. It was her art form. Dad loved it because they would work in the kitchen together when they had time. It was like a date night for them. My mouth waters every time I walk into the kitchen thinking of the garlic and herb aromas wafting through the house.

"Mom missed dad while he was in the navy. She worked very hard at the restaurant while he served.

"I was born when my father returned from the serving in the navy and was working in the restaurant. Shortly afterward they started the winery. When I was a teenager, I had no interest in the winery. My calling was to be a teacher, and I loved teaching. Now look at me back in the winery business anyway."

Kristy dialed her phone as she spoke to me. She tried to call her mother, but Bea's phone went immediately to voice mail. Sheriff and I dropped Kristy off at the winery and looked for Héctor.

Kristy later reported that she searched for her mother at the winery but could not find her anywhere.

"I went to mother's home. When I opened the door and called for mom, there was no answer. My heart sank."

As she searched the rooms, dreading to find her mother dead too, she felt a sense of relief when she found the house empty.

In her mother's bedroom, she was surprised to find an open, empty suitcase lying on the bed. Looking in the closet where her mom kept her luggage, Kristy found that the other suitcase was missing. Bea's car was not there. Kristy sensed that her mother left in great haste.

My cell phone rang. It was Kristy. "Where could my mother be? Mom would never leave an open suitcase on the bed unless she packed and ran out the door. She even left her medications in the bathroom.

"It is not like her to be away from my father. Mom was totally dedicated to Dad. They were never apart. Mom's absence is very suspicious.

"Mom has taken day trips before but never stayed overnight. She was very protective of my dad. Plus, it is strange that dad would be in the vineyard at night. His eyes were getting bad and he avoided being in dark places at night when he had difficulty seeing."

Kristy posted a $50,000 reward for information leading to the arrest of Oto's killer and information about the disappearance of Bea.

Sheriff Longo suspected Héctor knew more than he had first revealed. "I'm a big reader of peoples' attitudes. When I see someone not looking me in the eye, I become suspicious. When they look away avoiding eye contact or try to stare me down, I become even more suspicious.

"Héctor was fidgety. He wanted to leave and not make conversation. All of his answers were really brief. I noticed sweat on his brow and he started breathing heavily.

"I have known Héctor for a long time and he would always make conversation with me. When I questioned him this time, he acted like he did not even know me. Yes, there is more going on with Héctor than meets the eye."

We found Héctor by the agricultural shed. Sheriff asked him about Friday night.

Héctor told Sheriff Longo, "When I left work on Friday, Bea was in the tasting room pouring for some guests from Albania. They told her that they came to Argyle, Texas, after the Albanian/Serbian conflict in 1998-1999 and started a horse ranch training cutting horses.

"They were sorry that they could not meet Oto. Bea told them that Oto was scheduled to be on panels Saturday and Sunday at the Texas Wine and Grape Growers meeting in Grapevine about how to develop a VIP club and a wine ship program.

"I left work to take my wife to the Winstar casino and we spent the weekend playing slot machines.

She loves to gamble and has racked up a lot of debt with her gambling trips. She promised me she was going to stop. I went with her to make sure she did not go overboard.”

That still did not establish why Oto was in the vineyard and that Bea was alive this weekend working in the retail room. Bea was normally off on Monday and Tuesday.

Kristy opened the winery on Wednesday after getting home late Tuesday from California. I had promised Oto that I would work with Kristy on Wednesday. Even though she had only arrived the night before, she was there and ready for me Wednesday morning.

“Thank you for being here, Trevor. Please forgive me if I seem preoccupied. I cannot stop thinking about my dad’s murder and my mom’s disappearance.” She began to cry.

I did not really know what to do. I felt sorry for her but at the same time I knew that we needed to continue what Oto had requested us to do.

I tried to console her, “Kristy, I cannot imagine how hard this must be for you. So many losses in such a short time. Let’s focus on those things we can control. Perhaps it will take our minds off of those things we cannot control.”

As we worked together she had many questions that I tried to answer but I knew that what she

really wanted most was to have her mom and dad
by her side.

Chapter 8

Kristy's fiancé Mathew was well respected by her parents. Mathew was born in Serbia and brought to the United States with his family in 1999.

His father was a policeman in Serbia. Wounded by a sniper shot during a battle of Serbian and Albanian extremists, he was granted asylum to the United States.

Kristy shared that Mathew's Serbian first name was Mateja. That is translated Mathew in English.

Mathew was proud of his heritage and even taught Kristy how to make Banitsa, which was Mathew's favorite dessert. Banitsa is a traditional pastry that started in Bulgaria and spread to Serbia. It is a layered mixture of eggs, yogurt, brined cheese and filo pastry. It can be served hot or cold. Kristy taught Lulu and of course, I benefit.

Banitsa Recipe

Ingredients
- *1/2 cup butter, melted*
- *1/2 cup feta cheese, crumbled*
- *6-12 eggs (depending on how much you like eggs)*
- *7-ounce phyllo sheets*

Instructions

1. *Add the eggs and melted butter to a bowl and mix well together. Stir in the crumbled feta cheese.*

2. *Preheat your oven to 350F.*

3. *Grease an ovenproof pan with butter or line with parchment paper.*

4. *Add the first sheets of phyllo dough (Scrunch the phyllo dough. It looks a little accordion folded. It is about two phyllo sheets per layer.)*

5. *Spread the filling all over the phyllo layer in a thin layer. The feta crumbles can stay whole. Make sure to also get the corners and sides.*

6. *Add another layer or phyllo dough on top.*

7. *Continue until you run out of the egg mixture.*

8. *The top layer should be phyllo. Spread a few chunks of butter on top and sprinkle 1/2 cup of water all over.*

9. *Bake for about 30 minutes or until golden brown.*

It was surprising that Oto and Bea had never met Mathew's parents. The engagement happened very quickly while his parents vacationed in Serbia.

Mathew asked Kristy, "Have you heard from your mother? I am sure she will turn up."

Kristy appreciated that Mathew was trying to cheer her up. "No, I have not heard from her and I am worried."

Mathew repeated, giving her a side hug, "I am sure she is fine."

Kristy called Sheriff Longo, "I still have not heard from my mother. It is not like Mom to just take off. I want to file a missing person's report."

Sheriff Longo answered, "We will get right on it."

Kristy searched for clues in the winery office that might lead her to Bea. She noticed a map open to Texoma.

Then she became curious about the financial ledgers and at once immersed herself in the winery's books. She noticed that there was very little money in the bank account.

Their distributor owed them a lot of money. Oto had told Kristy he was thinking of changing distributors and suing the old distributor once they had made the move. Kristy noticed accounts receivable of $250,000 due from the distributor. They were more than six months old.

She then noticed that the winery's accounts payable was $400,000. Remembering that her mom told her January was the lowest revenue for most wineries, she rationalized that it could have been just because it was January.

Kristy could still see in her mind her mom saying, "When the bank account gets low, I spend every day calling accounts to get orders." She knew how to get orders in a bad month.

One check in particular caught Kristy's eye. It was a check written in December and signed by Oto Arrgos to John Hancock for life insurance.

Kristy's mom never mentioned buying a large insurance policy.

Kristy contemplated aloud, "Oto must have bought the insurance and told Bea not to tell me. Kristy surmised that her dad must have known that he had cancer and then rushed out to buy the insurance before the cancer appeared on his medical record.

"Mom and Dad were inseparable. If mom knew Oto was dead, then the kidnapper could have killed her. Or, what if mom could have taken her own life just to bail out the winery's terrible finances?!"

When Kristy called John Hancock, a representative told her the insurance only pays out when both her parents pass away. The representative also told Kristy that she was listed as the executrix and the beneficiary; and that the insurance agent who sold the policy had retired and moved out of town.

A sense of panic overcame Kristy as she quickly realized that she now owned a winery in bad financial shape, her dad and mentor was dead, her mother and confidante was missing. Her head started spinning and she felt dizzy as she tried to dial her phone.

Mathew answered and Kristy tearfully poured out her feelings and all the bad news to him speaking so fast Mathew could barely understand her.

"Mathew, I can't believe my father is dead. My mother is missing. My mother never leaves town without telling me. I found a map in the office opened to Texoma and then when I went to her house, I found an open suitcase on her bed. Then I looked in the closet and found another suitcase was missing. And her car is gone! Where do you think my mother went?"

He assured her that her mom would be found. "Kristy, I loved your dad. He was a great man. He had so much confidence in you. We will miss him together.

"Your mom loves you very much and she would never leave without telling you. The fact that there was an open suitcase and a map might show that she was thinking about going somewhere.

"She is probably visiting a friend in town. Let's start by going to some of Bea's favorite places. I'll drive. Where do you think she would go?"

Kristy thought out loud, "Mom loved to go to the local flower garden. It was always a place of peace and tranquility for her. I am sure that when she found out about Dad's death, she sought a peaceful place to think.

"Another place that she might go is to church so that she could pray for his soul and for her family's future. Mom would often pray to the Lord that He might put His wall of fire around us."

Mathew came to pick up Kristy and drove her to all of those places.

The first stop was the flower garden. There was the master gardener, Mike Vidrine, cleaning the beds in preparation of Spring planting. Kristy asked if he had seen Bea.

Mike said, "I have been working these gardens the last few days and have not seen your mother, Kristy. Is your mother missing?"

Not wanting to disclose the problem, Kristy answered, "I have just come back to town and was looking for her."

At the church they saw their pastor, Martin Brock. "I was so sorry to hear about Oto's passing," he said, "Please let me know if there is anything that I can do. Oto and Bea were such wonderful friends. I remember many delicious meals with them at their home. Oto will be missed. I have not seen Bea. Is she missing?"

Kristy shared, "I went to the house and she was not there."

Martin consoled her, "Kristy, you are going to need to give Bea a chance to grieve the loss of her husband of many years. It is not an easy process and grieving is different for each of us."

Kristy left the church and called me to see if I had heard from Bea. I responded, "No, is she still gone? I have not seen her but I will keep a look out for her."

Kristy sighed, "I am worried sick about her, but I need to get my focus on saving the winery. Can you join Mathew and me for dinner to discuss the plan to improve the vineyard? Why don't we meet at the Saltgrass Steakhouse?"

I was amazed how quickly Kristy's thoughts could move away from grief of her father's death to thinking about saving the winery.

"Can I bring Lulu?" I asked Kristy.

"Of course, I look forward to meeting her."

At dinner I was amazed how quickly Lulu and Kristy hit it off. I had never met Mathew before and found him to be very engaging. He appeared to care deeply for Kristy.

I briefed Kristy on the vineyard plan. When I told her it would take thirty-five thousand dollars to fix the vineyard, she almost flipped out. She said, "We do not have that kind of money! How am I going to get all the money?"

I felt so sorry for her. She was dealing with a lot. She seemed to be on a roller coaster of extremes, one minute laughing, the next minute crying and the next minute silently introspective.

We were there for three hours and had so much to discuss. Lulu got Kristy to share her experiences in New York. Mathew described his legal practice and his Serbian heritage. I had never met a person from Serbia. Lulu and Kristy talked nonstop. They seemed to have so much in common.

I thanked Kristy and Mathew for dinner, "The food and the service were outstanding. The wine we had was Messina Hof's Texas Hold'em. It was incredible. I looked up what grape varieties were in the Texas Hold'em and found it is a blend of some of my favorite grapes, Primitivo, Sagrantino, and Cabernet Sauvignon.

"It amazed me to read on the back label the history of the Texas Hold'em card game. Imagine, Amarillo Slim invented the game in Robstown, Texas. What a fitting wine to be on the wine list at a Texas steakhouse. I bet it is in all of the casinos in the USA."

It was particularly impressive how Mathew was so confident that Bea was okay and that he felt there was no reason to be upset. Kristy was so close to her mom and Mathew's assurances helped Kristy to cope with everything that had been thrown at her.

After we left the restaurant I told Lulu, "How could Mathew be so confident that Kristy's mother was okay?"

The thought crossed my mind, *'Could Mathew have kidnapped Bea? What would be Mathew's motive?'*

Chapter 9

Kristy was to meet with the winemaking consultant to go over protocols and taste through the wines in tank and in barrels. She was moving as fast as possible to prepare for the winemaker consultant while at the same time looking for her mother and arranging Oto's funeral services.

Lulu and I came to the winery and gave Kristy a written report so that she could share it with Héctor and ask him to postpone his retirement.

Kristy said, "Trevor, Lulu volunteered to help me in any way I see fit. I am very grateful that Lulu would come to my aide when I need it most.".

Kristy was trembling, so I told her, "Lulu and I are here for you."

Lulu at once started sorting through the mail and threw out all the junk. She then separated the bills, checks for wine payments, correspondence, and began to answer the phone while organizing the office.

As she was working and I was talking with Kristy, I saw Lulu pause. Her face clouded and she slowly lifted an envelope that appeared to be stained with a red liquid.

"Trevor, Kristy, look at this," she said. "On the back of this envelope is written, 'Oto, your time will come.'"

I took the envelope from her. It was obvious that the person who sent it was unaware that Oto was already dead.

"I will give this to Sheriff Longo so he can get it to the forensic lab."

Kristy looked shaken. She asked me, "What does this mean? Why would someone do this? Does this mean there was more than one person trying to hurt my family?"

Lulu immediately went to Kristy and put her arms around her.

"Kristy," Lulu whispered, "Do not worry. Trevor is here. I am here. The Lord is here with you."

Kristy sighed and said to Lulu, "Wow, you are such a helper! Thank you."

Lulu responded, "What else can I do to help?"

A smile crept across Kristy's face, "You can go out and get us lunch."

Lulu eagerly offered, "How about BBQ?"

Kristy chuckled and said, "That would be great."

It was good to see Kristy's face brighten even if only for a brief moment.

Kristy turned to me and said, "Trevor, this morning I received a phone call from an individual who was muffling his voice. He demanded a ransom payment for the release of mom! He told me to 'place $50,000 cash in a brown paper bag and put it in the Argyle Horse Farms mailbox at 7:00 pm tonight or I will never see Bea alive'.

"I told him that the winery does not have $50,000 and that it would take a day for me to raise that much money. What am I going to do?"

I echoed, "What are you going to do?"

Kristy responded, "I will have to take all the money out of my savings account to pay off the ransom. I hope we can catch the kidnapper. That money is the total of all my savings. I may have to use it to bail out the winery. First things first, I have to save my mother. Then I can shift my attention to saving the winery."

"You need to immediately call Sheriff Longo and tell him about the call," I encouraged, "Get him involved."

She called Sheriff Longo and shared the ransom demand with him. He said that he would call the FBI to help in the kidnapping investigation.

The FBI agent's name was Scott, and he arrived in Argyle that afternoon. Sheriff Longo and Agent Scott were old friends. At one time they were both police officers in the Argyle Police Department.

Sheriff Longo told me, "Scott is a straight up guy."

When Sheriff and Scott came to meet with Kristy and me, they expressed surprise that Bea was mentioned by name in the ransom call.

Scott remarked, "The kidnapper must have known who she was or talked with someone who knew her. It is also interesting that the kidnapper is aware of the Argyle Horse Farms."

Agent Scott asked Kristy, "Describe the kidnappers voice. Was it a familiar voice to you?"

Kristy took a moment to think about her answer, "It sounded like the person on the other end of the line was Hispanic and was speaking in broken English."

Scott asked, "Did the kidnapper request the money be in cash? Did he specify what type of cash? Why did he want the money placed in a mailbox at a horse farm?"

Kristy looked frazzled and fearful.

I said, "Let's pause and review what we now know. The kidnapper was probably a local Hispanic male who is familiar with the horse farm. The kidnapper knew Bea because they called her by name. The kidnapper believed the winery had $50,000 or would be coming into a large sum of money."

Agent Scott suggested, "Sheriff Longo tells me that you will have the $50,000. If so, when you get the money, we will record all the serial numbers of the bills.

"Then we apply to the bills a special die that is invisible to the naked eye. The die can be later detected using special equipment to confirm that the bills were part of the ransom. We can also put a tracking device in the bag which will allow us to follow the money in real time. This will assure us of recapturing your money after we capture the kidnapper.

"I must be upfront, Kristy, that there is always the chance that the kidnapper gets the money and escapes with it. It is unlikely and we will do everything we can to stop him, but you need to know the worst-case scenario."

He tapped her on the shoulder in respect and said, "I think our next stop is the Argyle Horse Farm."

On the way to the horse farm, Kristy expressed concern but added, "Well, at least it appears that my mother is still alive."

At the horse farm they met the owner, Tom Plant.

Agent Scott asked Tom if he had any Hispanic employees. Tom said, "All of my employees are Hispanic. Why do you ask?"

"We are investigating a potential kidnapping. Can I have a list of all your Hispanic employees?"

Tom was very cooperative and shared the list. He added, "You know, Kristy, many of my employees go to the winery on Fridays after work and are familiar with your employees.

"They talk about your guests frequently. The Albanians last Friday were favorites because my employees knew them from another horse farm nearby."

I asked Tom what time his workers got off on Fridays.

He answered, "Between 5 and 6 pm. It is the end of the work week and loose ends on the farm must be completed before they can leave."

I noticed four of Tom's employees had sequential social security numbers and was suspicious that they had provided falsified identification. They were all new to Argyle and Argyle had a huge influx of illegal aliens that entered through the Texas/Mexico border. Argyle's very large Hispanic population makes it easier for them to disappear into the population.

"Tom," I asked, "Do you have any documents that show their handwriting?"

While Tom went to gather the documents, I told Sheriff Long that I wanted to compare the handwriting to the threatening letter Kristy received.

Sheriff Long responded, "Trevor, you really are an investigator. I like the way you think."

Tom returned with the documents.

On the way back to the office, Agent Scott told Sheriff, "It will take a while to put all these names in the FBI database to see if any of these people have a record."

Chapter 10

Kristy called Héctor and me into her office. "Héctor, I need to ask you to postpone your retirement. The winery needs you."

Héctor seemed angry that she would ask him this, especially since she hired me to oversee the vineyard. Héctor would be working for me. Oto had worked alongside Héctor and respected Héctor's knowledge. Héctor would have to learn to respect mine.

"Hi, Héctor," I interjected quickly, "I have prepared a manual for the vineyard from which we can work. I reviewed the soil sample reports, water sample reports, and the leaf analysis reports over the last year. These are my recommendations."

Héctor looked through the manual silently. He closed the book and looking at me, said with some hostility, "You changed the spray program, the fertilization plan, and the irrigation schedule. Why?"

Patiently, I explained the how and why of this plan. "The vineyard yielded only one and one-half tons per acre last year and the yields had been declining over the past three years.

"I noticed there were no petiole samplings at bloom or at veraison. These reports normally dictate the fertilization program for the coming season."

Héctor argued that he had been using fish emulsion on the vineyard for more than twenty years.

"Yes, I saw that but also noticed the emulsion had very low nitrogen, phosphorus, and potassium. All three of these components are essential for plant growth and crop yield. The emulsion was not enough.

"Plus, the irrigation was limited to once every ten days. The last three years Argyle has experienced the worst drought in twenty years. The vineyard has a lot of sand, so irrigating every ten days was okay with normal rainfall but in a drought condition irrigation has to be increased to every five days for twelve hours.

"The records showed that you were spraying for powdery mildew, but in North Texas downy mildew is more likely the cause for poor leaf coverage."

After I explained everything to Héctor, he lowered his eyes as though embarrassed. His shoulders relaxed and he seemed much more receptive. Héctor then told Kristy that he would postpone his retirement.

After Héctor left the office, I turned to Kristy and said, "I thought that went well." She seemed to relax. Her shoulders dropped in relief as she smiled and agreed.

Kristy's phone rang. She answered. A man with a muffled voice began to talk. Kristy immediately put her phone on speaker.

The voice on the other end of the phone demanded payment and said, "When are you putting the money in the mailbox?"

Kristy quickly responded, "Let me speak with my mother. I am not putting the money in the mailbox until I speak with my mother. I have to know that she is alive."

The caller abruptly hung up the phone. Kristy tried to call back, but the line was dead.

She commented, "This voice sounded the same as the first caller."

I thought out loud, "The kidnapper may have been the person who killed Oto or someone who heard that Bea was missing. Secondly, the kidnapper may have known that Oto had just bought a large insurance policy. Thirdly, the kidnapper's refusal to have Bea get on the phone is not a good sign."

Kristy looked worried, "Who knew that Oto bought a large insurance policy when Dad did not even tell me? Do you think it could have been the insurance agent that retired?"

We called Sheriff Longo and filled him in on the insurance policy, the second call, and our suspicions. Sheriff Longo agreed and said that he and Scott were on their way to the winery.

I joined FBI agent Scott and Sheriff Longo to interview all the employees of the vineyard and winery. They were also getting the names of all the people who had access to keys of the 4-wheeler who were working in the vineyard on Friday.

The first person to be interviewed was Héctor.

"Héctor, I understand you found the body on Monday and that you were in the vineyard on Friday, the day they think Oto was killed," stated Scott.

"Further, you had access to the 4-wheeler. You said you were retiring because you heard from Oto that a vineyard consultant was going to be making changes in the vineyard. It sounds like you might have been the last person to see Oto alive. What can you tell us about that encounter?"

Héctor seemed very nervous saying, "Remember that I left Friday right after work to take my wife to the casino in Oklahoma. Many people had access to the 4-wheeler. All the vineyard, winery, and retail department had access to the keys.

"The 4-wheeler is also used to take the trash to the dumpster each evening and to pull customers out of the mud when their cars get stuck after a large rain.

"All of the vineyard workers were in the vineyard on Friday. It is pruning season. I dismissed them early after they had forty hours."

Sheriff Longo asked, "Where did you stay in Oklahoma?"

Héctor responded, "At the casino hotel."

Sheriff Longo continued, "I understand you are retiring. Is there a reason you are retiring now?"

"I was retiring because my wife is retiring and we were planning to travel. Kristy told me that the winery needs me and asked me not to retire. I have now agreed to stay."

Sheriff Longo congratulated Héctor on not retiring but added, "That must have been a hard decision. I understand that you and Oto were very close."

Héctor looked sad, "Oto treated me like family. I drove Oto into town when he went to see his doctor. We just went last month. Oto was very organized. He also saw his lawyer and his insurance agency, John Hancock, on the same day."

Scott looked curious, "That seems like a lot to do in one day. Did he do that often?"

"No, but all of his providers are in one building. The offices are located in a 4-story professional office complex in downtown Argyle. There were attorneys, doctors, insurance companies, financial planners, and accountants all officed in the same building.

"Oto was in the offices for almost two hours. When he returned to the car, Oto told me that he felt much better about the future of the winery. But he was in a cold sweat. When I asked if he was ok, he said he was relieved and the winery was financially set. Not understanding why he would be in a cold sweat if the winery were financially set, I asked Oto what "set" meant.

"He smiled at me and said, 'I just bought an insurance policy that will help make the winery secure.'"

Scott said, "So, that was the only time you took him to see all three businesses at once?"

Héctor replied, "Yes, but one day when I was sick, my assistant vineyard manager, José, drove Oto to the doctor and he may have taken him to see all three."

Sheriff Longo asked, "What attorney did Oto meet with?"

Héctor said he did not know.

"What financial planner?

"I do not know. I waited downstairs. Oto did say that all three businesses were on the third floor."

Chapter 11

Next, we interviewed all of the vineyard crew. When asked where they were on Friday, they all said they finished their forty hours by 2:00 pm so Héctor and all six of them left. They confirmed that Héctor put the 4-wheeler in front of retail and left the key in the ignition to make it easier for the retail staff to use that evening.

Sheriff Longo interviewed José. "José, have you ever taken Oto to the doctor's office?"

José responded, "I did take Oto to the doctor's office last month when Héctor was sick, and he also went to the insurance agency and the attorney's office."

"Did Oto tell you why he went there?"

José quickly said "no," then he asked if he could get back to the vineyard.

I could tell the sheriff did not believe José. Sheriff Longo looked at me and gave me a double wink.

Sheriff asked José, "How was the relationship between Héctor and Oto?"

"I think it was okay. Héctor liked Oto very much."

"José, when was the last time you saw Bea?"

"I saw her Friday when I picked up my check before going home."

"What did you do Friday night, José?"

"I took my wife to the Lone Star track to watch the horse races. My wife loves horses. She rode all the time as a child. It is one of the things she loved about Argyle – all the horse farms."

Héctor walked back into the room after José left and said, "The retail manager uses the 4-wheeler to take the garbage to the dumpster at the end of the day."

Sheriff then interviewed the retail manager who said, "I used the 4-wheeler at 10:00 pm on Friday to remove the garbage when we locked up. The dumpster is located in the parking lot. It is on the other side of the property from the vineyard."

Sheriff Longo asked, "Was there anything strange about the 4-wheeler?"

The retail manager paused, "I did notice a dent in the back bumper and there was mud all over the passenger seat. Friday was a very busy night, so I did not notice anyone using the 4-wheeler. It would have been very easy. The key was left in the ignition."

"Who else was on property that night?" asked Sheriff.

The retail manager replied, "I had thirty local attorneys going on a winery tour that I conducted. And Bea hosted a group of local Albanian horse farm owners."

The coroner had told Sheriff Longo and me that Oto was killed between 5:00 pm-9:00 pm on Friday evening. So, it could have been one of the attorneys who were on the tour.

The retail manager continued, "The attorneys arrived at 5:45 pm and the tour started at 6:30 pm and ended at 7:30 pm. After that they were on their own - buying tastings and making purchases from retail. Almost everyone bought two or three bottles. Three of the attorneys bought a case each. One of them said he had won a big trial and was feeling rich."

Sheriff Longo asked, "Did you recognize any of them?"

"All three of the attorneys that bought cases were familiar to me," said the retail manager. "All three are platinum VIPs of the winery.

"One of them, Sal, told me that he was Kristy's senior prom date and that they dated for twelve months.

"The second one is named Danny. He is the district attorney. Oto and Bea supported him during his campaign.

"The third attorney is Kristy's fiancé, Mathew Koreni. He is a big supporter of the winery and even volunteers in retail here on his days off. He can work the register and has even closed up when I was tied up with employee duties.

"I know that Mathew knows how to drive the 4-wheeler because he has taken out the garbage at the end of a shift. He did tell me once that he hoped Oto would not interfere in his plans to marry Kristy."

I asked why Oto would interfere. The retail manager paused as though to decide whether to share more details. Sheriff Longo stepped toward her and looked at her with laser focus, "You do realize that we are talking murder here, right?"

She immediately shared, "Mathew said that Oto was very protective of Kristy and that Oto had not taken the time to get to know him. He seemed resentful that Oto knew Danny better and spent time with Danny. Kristy and Mathew never had dinner with Oto and Bea."

Sheriff Longo thanked her and left to interview the three attorneys. He looked at me and said, "I wonder if any of these attorneys have an office on the third floor."

We drove to the Argyle office complex and found that the only law firm on the third floor was Michael and Michael.

Chapter 12

The first attorney we interviewed was Sal.

Sal explained, "Kristy and I dated for the entire senior year of high school. We were the King and Queen for the senior prom. I proposed marriage but Kristy was not ready. We gradually grew apart."

Sheriff Longo sensed that Sal was still angry about the breakup.

Sal shared, "We occasionally run into each other, but the love seems to be gone. I have never given up on my relationship with Kristy. I even visited her in New York when she was teaching there.

"I took her to the Metropolitan Museum and proposed marriage again. Again, Kristy said no. You know, Oto never liked me. He poisoned Kristy's attitude about me. I have never been able to impress Oto."

Sheriff Longo then interviewed Danny. "It is good to see you again, Danny. I have a few questions that you may be able to help me with."

Danny nodded and replied, "Before we get started, I want to tell you how shocked I was to hear about Oto's death. Do you know who killed Oto?"

Sheriff responded, "Not yet but we are making great progress."

Danny said, "Great. I look forward to prosecuting this case.

"I was very disappointed when I did not see Oto while on tour Friday. I have fond memories of tasting wines with Oto in the wine lab. He told me that he enjoyed my comments because my opinion represented the average male wine consumer."

Sheriff Longo snickered but then became serious, "Danny are you aware that Bea is missing?"

Danny replied, "I had heard that and wondered where she might be. What have you heard about her?"

Sheriff Longo told Danny that the FBI was now involved.

Danny added, "I want you to know that, as a friend of the family, I hope to be as much help to Bea and Kristy as I can. I believe that Bea was planning a trip to visit a friend in Denison."

Next Sheriff Longo interviewed Mathew, Kristy's fiancé. "Mathew, it is good to see you again. Kristy is going to need you now more than ever. What is your relationship with Sal?"

Mathew replied, "I do not like him. He keeps harassing Kristy and asking her to marry him even though he knows she is engaged to me. Sal is obsessed."

Sheriff continues, "How do you feel about Danny?"

Mathew says, "Danny was my roommate in law school. We spent a lot of time together. He was one of my best friends. Kristy even looks upon him as a big brother."

"The retail manager mentioned that you are very protective of Kristy because she is very independent and takes a lot of risks. She said you were shocked that she took a teaching job in a risky neighborhood in the Bronx. Did you resent Danny? How well were you getting along with Oto?" asked Sheriff Longo.

Mathew looked surprised and stuttered, "Well, my relationship with Oto got off to a rocky start but was improving. Oto was very protective of Kristy. He distanced himself from me while spending more time with Danny. I did understand that Danny was one of his attorneys."

Then he asked Mathew, "Where were you on Friday night after the tour?"

Mathew said, "I was shopping for Kristy's wedding ring."

Sheriff Longo questioned, "Where did you go shopping?"

"Don Reiser Jewelers."

Sheriff Longo then asked, "Mathew, have you ever driven the 4-wheeler?"

Mathew said, "On a few occasions I helped retail close up and sometimes took out the trash with the 4-wheeler."

"Did you ever see someone else other than staff driving the 4-wheeler?"

"I saw Danny driving the 4-wheeler when he worked on the court case representing the winery. When Arrgos Cellars was first established, they trademarked the name. Five years ago, a new winery in Argyle took the name R Gos Cellars. Oto sued and Danny was the winery's attorney. He won a large judgement against the new winery.

"One day, I also saw Sal and Kristy driving around in the 4-wheeler having a serious conversation about something."

Sheriff Longo thanked Mathew for his information and then went to question Kristy.

"Kristy, why were you and Sal driving around in the 4-wheeler?"

Kristy looked irritated, "Sal had heard that I was getting engaged and he wanted to see if there was any chance we could get back together.

"I said no. Sal got angry and started driving the 4-wheeler very recklessly. That was the last time I saw Sal. He has called me at least three times, but I did not pick up.

"Sal thinks Oto's opinion of him was the reason I did not wish to marry Sal. Sal is very persistent, but I do not think he is capable of killing my dad or kidnapping my mom."

Sheriff Longo then asked, "Has Danny ever driven the 4-wheeler?"

Kristy replied, "Danny drove my dad around the vineyard discussing the court case. Anytime Dad was stressed, he preferred to be in the vineyard to relieve his stress.

"So, when they discussed the court case they would drive around the vineyard. Danny had a lot of serious matters concerning the court case, and the vineyard was the best place to do it."

Sheriff Longo then asked, "Did Mathew ever work in retail and help close up?"

Kristy said. "When Mathew came to pick me up at the end of the day, he helped in retail while he waited for me to finish up my work. I knew Mathew would throw out the trash and could use the 4-wheeler."

Then Sheriff Longo questioned Kristy, "Did you know where Mathew was on the Friday Oto was murdered?"

She shared, "I was attending a short course at University of California at Davis. We did not get out of class until 6:00 pm Pacific time which is 8:00 pm central time.

As the sheriff left, Kristy inquired, "Is Mathew a suspect?"

He paused, "I am sorry Kristy, everyone is a suspect until we solve this horrible murder and kidnapping."

Sheriff Longo went to the jewelry store. He asked the store owner about Mathew coming in to buy Kristy's engagement ring. Mr. Rieser said, "Yes, Mathew came in at 8:00 pm and left by 8:30 pm and he did, in fact, buy a ring. It was a beautiful heart-shaped diamond. Those are rare and quite expensive. I was surprised that he paid cash and had that much cash on him.

"He told me he had important business and had to get back to the winery. I thought he was in a hurry to pick up Kristy."

Sheriff Longo's phone rang. He picked up. It was me.

"Sorry to bother you, but I went back out where Oto was killed and found a newspaper article announcing Danny's run for District Attorney. I found it covered in mud in a deep tire track. You will probably want to see this."

I told Sheriff Longo and FBI agent Scott that Kristy was on the phone with me from 8:00 pm-8:30 pm the night of Oto's death.

"I was talking with Kristy about the vineyard plan. Kristy is attentive and had many questions for me. She was concerned about how much money it would take to fix the vineyard.

"Kristy was very excited about her short course at UC Davis."

Chapter 13

We later regrouped at the winery to review the evidence. While we were there, the coroner called Sheriff Longo. He asked if all of us could come down to the morgue. He had some very interesting new findings.

Sheriff Longo and I drove to the morgue in downtown Argyle. FBI agent Scott met us there. On the way to the morgue, I told the sheriff that Kristy was very concerned about winery finances.

"It seems that the winery cannot cover its bills. I am investigating some grant monies that might be available to help out.

"If Bea is unfortunately dead, of course, the insurance policy will pay off and there will be no need for the grants. But hopefully Bea is alive."

The morgue was in the cold, dimly lit basement of the old police station. The coroner greeted us, "I first thought Oto was killed when the 4-wheeler ran over him, but I discovered that Oto was struck in the head by a blunt object and run over more than once with the 4-wheeler.

"So, Oto probably knew his killer and may have had a face-to-face conversation that led to violence, which led to his death."

Sheriff Longo repeated what the coroner had said to make sure he understood, "Then the killer knocked out Oto with a blunt object and then ran over him more than once with the 4-wheeler."

The coroner confirmed.

I then reminded Sheriff that I had found the newspaper article about Danny running for District Attorney.

Immediately they all said Danny might be the killer but why? Oto had supported him for District Attorney. Why would Danny want to kill Oto?

Sheriff thought out loud, "Oto must have had the article, not Danny. Danny was friends with Kristy and was loved by Oto and Bea. Why would Oto have an old newspaper about Danny in the vineyard?"

I suggested that we look at the newspaper again to see what else might be in it. Once back in the evidence room at the Sheriff's office, we pulled out the newspaper.

As we unfolded the paper and put it down on the desk, it fell open to the second page. There inside the same newspaper it was reported that Héctor had been imprisoned in Dallas for attempted manslaughter.

Sheriff Longo asked me to talk to Héctor, "Héctor knows more than he has told us. And now we need to know what that old newspaper was doing in the vineyard."

The next day I showed up in the vineyard. Héctor was not there. I asked José, the assistant vineyard manager, where Héctor was.

José said, "Since early December Héctor comes in late and leaves early. He also spends a lot of time in town picking up supplies. He used to make a list and go into town one time per week. Now he goes into town almost every day. His work attitude and dedication have really changed.

"Mr. Talan, when Héctor retires, am I going to be promoted to vineyard manager?"

I was surprised that José did not know Héctor was not retiring, and I was not about to be the one to tell him.

"That is not for me to decide, José, that will be Kristy's decision."

José continued, "Héctor also said he went into town to keep his eye on his wife. She was retiring so she was going to have a lot of free time.

"Héctor is a very jealous man. His wife is a beautiful woman and he believed she was having an affair. Stella is ambitious. She told him she is tired of living the life of a vineyard manager's wife.

"Oto told me that Héctor's wife was spending time with Danny. She was his election secretary. On her time off from the bar, she made calls getting contributions. Danny's wife passed away and he found Stella cooperative and helpful.

"Héctor did not know what to believe. He decided to confront his wife. She claimed that she was loyal to him and had not had an affair."

I called Sheriff Longo with the new information. "Trevor, we have too many suspects and need to eliminate some of them."

I asked if I could help reduce the number of suspects. He said yes and I was delighted to assist.

On the way to his office, I went to the winery office to see Lulu. She is very intuitive. To my surprise Lulu had new information. She had gone into town and ran into Sal, Danny, and Mathew.

"I want to hear all about it," I told her, "but I have to meet with Sheriff Longo now. Let's go out later, Okay?"

She nodded, "Just one thing to know before you go, Héctor's wife told Danny she had met someone online from California and was thinking of leaving Héctor.

"She was fearful of Héctor's temper. When she did tell him, he did not believe her. They slept in separate bedrooms and argued often. She rarely cooked for Héctor and Héctor ate out all the time."

Chapter 14

When I arrived at Sheriff Longo's office, the sheriff was writing on his chalkboard. He wrote motive, opportunity, and means. The following people had some or all of these factors.

Héctor, Bea, Mathew, Sal, and José.

"Bea could not have done it." Sheriff began, "She is still missing and may be dead. She was devoted to Oto and could never harm him.

"Sal was not a supporter of Oto. Oto never supported his relationship with Kristy. Kristy's rejection of Sal ended his benefit of Oto's death.

"Sal had no knowledge of Oto's routine, so he is eliminated as a strong suspect."

The sheriff continued his observations, "The FBI found the insurance agent living in Grand Caymen. The insurance policy found in his apartment stipulated that the beneficiary and executrix is Kristy; and that the 10-million-dollar payout is when both of her parents pass away. No insurance is paid at Oto's death. The disappearance of Bea is now ever so important.

"The insurance agent apologized and said that he sent the policy by regular mail but should have sent the policy by registered mail.

"He said he was sorry to hear of Oto's death and Bea's absence and gave his condolences. So, he is no longer a suspect.

"Mathew, as Kristy's fiancé, had much to gain if Kristy's parents died after they married. If Bea died before they married, then the 10-million-dollar benefit would be in Kristy's estate. If Bea's death was discovered after they married, then the insurance payment would become an asset of the marriage and both parties would own the money.

"Mathew is a successful attorney and his family is very wealthy. He signed a prenup with Kristy. In either case he would not receive any part of the 10 million dollars. So, he had no motive.

"Kristy was on the phone with Trevor that night. So, she had no opportunity. She was studying in California.

"That leaves Héctor, José or an unidentified assailant of which we are not currently aware."

I shared, "Mathew has been pushing Kristy to move up the wedding date. He stated it was because he wanted to protect her and thought he could be more helpful as her husband."

Sheriff Longo looked at me with suspicious doubt.

"Kristy said she was focused on finding her mother and getting the winery on a good footing and out of financial distress before the wedding,"

I advocated. "She declined his pressure to move up the date."

I called Kristy and told her the insurance agent was found in the Caymen Islands, that the insurance policy was in the mail, and that she should be receiving it. That made Kristy work even harder to find her mother.

When I got home, Lulu was ready to go. "BBQ Tonight!" she said with a big smile on her face. "Let's go to 407 BBQ and I can tell you all about my interesting day."

When we arrived at the restaurant and placed our order, Lulu launched into the details of her day, "I went into town and saw Sal. He was on his way out of town and told me it looks like Kristy has made up her mind and is going to marry Mathew, so there is no hope for Kristy and him to get together. He seemed sad but resolved. He is pining lost love."

"Then, I ran into Danny at the grocery store. He said that he was heartbroken about Oto's death but was confident that they would soon find Bea."

"Why do you think he said 'soon'?" Lulu asked.

"It could just be his way of encouraging her," I answered.

She continued, "He also told me that the night of the murder, he had seen water running out of a vineyard row all the way down to the winery. He thought there might be a broken water line. I don't know if that helps but could be a clue.

"Then, when I was walking past the jewelry shop I saw Mathew who said he was there to get Kristy's wedding ring sized."

She stopped and looked at me, "What?"

I laughed.

"You are impressed with my detective work, aren't you?" She laughed.

My conversation with Lulu gave me a new theory about why Oto was in the vineyard the night of his death.

Chapter 15

There was a broken valve in the vineyard row where his body lay. He must have discovered the irrigation system was broken at that valve and went out to turn off the water. The killer saw him there and hit him with the large grapevine trunk.

What if Héctor was doing his vineyard check, saw Oto where the broken valve was, and Oto asked why it was not repaired? What if Oto reprimanded Héctor for leaving the valve broken and Héctor got angry? What if Héctor asked Oto about his share of the winery in the new will? What if Oto was showing Héctor the article about the attempted manslaughter and jail time? There were so many possibilities.

I asked Kristy if Héctor had reported the broken valve and how it happened. Kristy was unaware because she had been in California at the UC Davis course.

I then spoke to Héctor, who said, "One of the vineyard workers ran over the valve with the tractor. I did not tell Oto about the valve and I guess Oto discovered the broken valve the night he was killed."

I asked, "Isn't it normal that when the irrigation is broken that you immediately fix it?"

Héctor replied, "I was fixing it."

"So, when were you fixing it?" I asked.

Héctor looked away, "I fixed it on Friday."

"So, you were in the vineyard late Friday afternoon or evening? Did you see Oto?

"You said you left early to go to the casino with your wife. Your team said you left at 2 pm. But, you said you saw the Albanians. They did not come to the winery until 6 pm."

Héctor fidgeted, "Yes, I saw Oto."

"Was Oto alive when you left him?"

Héctor said, "Of course he was."

I did not believe what Héctor said. His body language was closed with his arms folded in front of him. He did not look me in the eye and he was breathing rapidly. His left eye twitched when he talked. He had obviously lied about the time he left the vineyard.

I continued, "What about the newspaper I found in the vineyard? When we opened it at the Sheriff's office, it fell to a page that featured an article about you being put in jail for trying to kill someone. What happened?"

Héctor was visibly shaken, "I was at a bar in Dallas with Stella. She was flirting right in front of me with another man at the bar. Winking and laughing she strutted her stuff back and forth for all to see.

"I had a little too much to drink and could not contain myself. One minute I was sitting at the bar being ignored by my wife, and the next minute I was being pulled out of a fight by the police, taken to jail, and my face plastered in the newspaper.

"Oto did not know about the arrest until he saw the newspaper when my wife dropped it off at his office. My wife was so angry at me that she took the newspaper to Oto to hurt me."

My phone rang. It was Kristy interrupting my conversation with Héctor. Embarrassed and angry, he took off as soon as I answered the phone.

"Mathew and I are going out to dinner. Would you and Lulu like to join us?"

At dinner, Kristy shared, "It is so nice to take a break from all this turmoil. Thank you all for being so supportive and helpful. I am hopeful we will find Mom.

"Once we do find her, I can't wait to start planning the wedding. It will help take my mind off of the murder investigation and the winery problems.

"There is one thing that I want to ask. Lulu, you have become like a sister to me. Would you be my Maid of Honor?"

Lulu was delighted to accept.

I did not have the heart to share any of the investigation updates. It was a great repose from the turmoil.

The next day, Sheriff Longo asked Kristy if she knew where Bea could have gone, "Did Oto and Bea own property other than their home or winery?"

Kristy said, "Oto and Bea owned rent houses that many of the employees rented. Here are the addresses. All but one of the houses are rented. One is empty. Héctor's oldest son was renting it but moved out. He recently got married and moved into a larger apartment."

Sheriff Longo called me to go with him to the empty rent house. We found the front door open.

"Food was in the refrigerator. The heater was left off. It was below freezing in the house. As we went room to room, we found no one. In the closet we found some of Héctor's clothes.

I told Sheriff, "It seems Héctor moved in when his son moved out. Perhaps Héctor's marital troubles are worse than we thought."

From there we went to Héctor's house to speak with him. When we arrived, Héctor's wife said she and Héctor got into a terrible fight, and Héctor stormed off. She did not know where he was.

The sheriff put out word to his men to be on the lookout for Héctor. Swiftly they found him at the Star Lounge by one of Sheriff's officers. Héctor was drunk.

The officer reported that Héctor was mumbling, *"Oto was a good man... Oto was a good man… Why was he in the vineyard? Why was he in the vineyard? My wife is leaving me… She is moving to California… She has a new love… What will I do without her? I will be all alone… My life is over."*

Weeping uncontrollably, Héctor did not even put up a fight as he was arrested. He was a broken man.

When he sobered up, he admitted he saw Oto in the vineyard on Friday night. "When Oto showed me the newspaper article, I told him it was just a big misunderstanding. I expected that the assault charges would be dropped."

I thought about how many changes were happening in Héctor's life and all that he was experiencing.

One day he was the vineyard boss and now he has to follow orders. His beautiful wife is leaving him for a new lover. The winery where he spent much of his adult life is now in trouble and the new owner knows little about growing grapes or making wine.

Life is full of surprises. Everything changes in time. One minute we can be on top of the world and the next minute in the dumps. Love and hate can change so fast.

Anger can take control of one's life and make us do things that we regret. We never know what tomorrow will bring.

Chapter 16

I went back to the vineyard to look for clues that we or the police may have missed. Channeling what might have happened in the vineyard that night, I could feel that Oto knew his attacker and that he and his attacker were purposefully meeting in the vineyard.

I walked up and down the rows. The sun must have set when this meeting occurred. That night was windy and dark.

Oto had an event that night, so he had to believe it was urgent for him to leave the winery to see someone in the vineyard. He took the newspaper with him. He must have seen his attacker as he walked toward him in the vineyard.

The attacker must have come from the opposite direction and been standing in the vineyard facing the winery. Oto was elderly but strong in stature. His hands were rough – the hands of a vinetender. He was no longer quick of foot.

As I backtracked further into the vineyard in a path that the attacker might have taken, I shined my flashlight at the vineyard. There was a patch of disturbed ground and some damage to a vine. It looked like there may have been a physical altercation.

The light from the flashlight illuminated something shiny catching my eye. It was a necklace tangled in the damaged vine. In the weeds, there was a pruning shear and grafting knife. In my heart, I knew these must have belonged to someone who worked in the vineyard and was the killer.

Suddenly, when I raised the flashlight, a man's figure was illuminated. Then, I felt a blow to my head. It knocked me out. When I came to, I was alone and my assailant had vanished into the night. I was not even sure how long I had been out. Slowly and wabbly I made my way back to my car.

I called Sheriff Longo and asked him to meet me at the jail where Héctor was staying. We arrived at the same time. I showed Sheriff what I found in the vineyard.

Sheriff Longo looked at me and asked, "What happened to you? Your head is bleeding."

I told him what happened to me in the vineyard and that I suspected Héctor, but he was in jail.

"Héctor, can you please identify these items for me?"

Héctor stared and spoke slowly, "They belong to me. I had lost them. I thought one of the vineyard crew took them from my locker. My tools have been missing for two weeks. José is trying to get my job. Thank you for finding them and returning them to me."

"I found these in the vineyard near the place where Oto was killed. Can you please explain how they got there?"

"José must have taken them from my locker and threw them in the vineyard to make it seem like I lost them there."

"That's interesting," I baited, "We already talked to José. According to him, your recent behavior has been full of anger toward Oto and Bea because you resented the fact that they hired a vineyard consultant.

"He immediately identified your pruning shears and grafting knife. He even showed us where you had carved your initials in the handle," as I pointed to the carvings.

"José said he did not take them. He also shared that he saw you with your tools on Friday.

"He also said the necklace belonged to your wife. She wore it all the time."

"José wants my job," insisted Héctor, "He planted these things in the vineyard."

Héctor became emotional, "Oto was my friend but I was betrayed by him.

"Oto and Bea screwed me! Years ago, they promised me a part of the winery in their original will. It was a reward for my hard work and loyalty. I loved them like my own family and gave everything I had to their business. My dedication even cost me my wife. She was sick and tired of being married to a lowly vineyard worker. Oto and Bea owed me!"

Héctor fumed, "Then I learned that Oto and Bea had created a new will making Kristy the beneficiary and executrix. I was not even mentioned in the will. Kristy is getting everything.

"You showed up, Trevor, because Oto hired you to be the boss. I went from boss to working for you. You don't even know this vineyard.

"I designed it alone, cared for it all those years, and have a vision for what it could be. I would have done much more but every time I wanted to buy new equipment Oto rejected the request.

"I was so angry. I told him that he owed me an explanation and that I could not wait. He needed to come to the vineyard now.

"I was just going to talk with him, but as he walked toward me, I got angrier and angrier. Oto had a quick pace. He waved a newspaper above his head."

'Hurry up, Héctor', Otto said. 'Why did I have to find out about you being in jail through a newspaper? When were you going to tell me? This is attempted murder!

'And why am I finding you in the vineyard fixing an irrigation valve? You and I need to talk but I can't right

now because I have to get back to the winery. I have some important guests.'

Héctor continued, "I accused him of not being interested in what I had to say.

"*'How could you betray me?!'* I charged. *"You promised me a part of the vineyard. You seem to have forgotten, Oto, all of your promises to me."*

"Oto told me, *'Héctor, you have been an important member of our team. We appreciate you but you need to think of the future of the winery and Kristy. We are in trouble and close to bankruptcy. If we let it continue as before, there would be nothing left for anyone. Besides, you may be facing jail time for attempted manslaughter! You can't be much help to Kristy if you are sitting in jail.'*

"That just made my blood boil. My emotions took control over me. I could not stand it anymore," sighed Héctor, "*'nothing left for anyone'.* It sounded like there would be something for Kristy. Why not me? Oto was only looking out for Kristy's future and had no regard for my future.

"In a rage, I grabbed a dead grapevine trunk that had been pruned earlier that week and hit Oto, knocking him down. When he got up to walk away, I jumped on the 4-wheeler and backed up. I felt a thump. I realized I had backed over Oto.

"My back wheel was stuck in the mud. I panicked and put the gear into forward and ran over Oto again. I heard the same loud thump. Still stuck I continued to run the 4-wheeler back and forth until it was freed. I quickly sped off and parked the 4-wheeler in front of retail. I must have left the key in the ignition."

Héctor began to weep. As we left I asked, "Héctor, where is Bea?"

He shrugged his shoulders and murmured, "I have not seen her since Friday. By the way, José was bragging about coming into a large sum of money.

"When I hired José, I knew he had spent time in jail. He had stolen money from the Catholic Church. On a Saturday, he broke into the Contrition box – you know where you put money to gain entrance into heaven.

"He stole one hundred fifty dollars. He was a teenager from a broken home so he spent twelve months in juvenile detention. José had a mother who was a drunk and a father who took off right after José was born."

Sheriff Longo and I went to Josés house and questioned him about where he was going to get a large sum of money.

José laughed, "I was only bragging. Did Héctor tell you what I said?"

Sheriff Longo asked for Josés cell phone. When José handed his phone over, I noticed there was another cell phone on the dining room table and retrieved it.

Sheriff Longo looked at the first cell phone. There were very few calls. He looked up at José and asked about his calls. José had good answers for each call.

I asked, "What about the second cell phone?"

José shrugged his shoulders and responded, "I just keep it in case of an emergency."

That further increased the sheriff's interest and he asked if he could review the calls.

José fidgeted uneasily and said, "I have not made any calls in more than a month on that phone."

Sheriff Longo replied, "Well, then I guess you would not mind if I take a look at it."

José reluctantly nodded approval.

I handed the phone to Sheriff Longo. He looked at it and said, "The last two calls on this phone were to Kristy. Why would you be calling Kristy? And why was one call one minute twenty seconds and the other only twenty-five seconds?"

I could tell José knew that he had been caught. He said, "I told Kristy that I could find Bea and that I would get the $50,000 reward money."

Kristy had already told Sheriff Longo and me that the two calls she received were ransom calls claiming to have kidnapped Bea. Sheriff Longo then said to José, "Take me to where Bea is."

José began to fidget again and sweat poured down his face.

Sheriff commanded, "Get in the car, José, and take us to Bea."

José broke down and said he had no idea where Bea was. "Since Bea was missing I thought I could call Kristy, say that I was a kidnapper, and take advantage of Bea's disappearance. I could collect $50,000 easy money."

Sheriff Longo then said, "José, why did you attack Trevor in the vineyard?"

José responded, "I took Héctor's wife's necklace and his vineyard tools into the vineyard. Trevor caught me. I had no choice. So, I knocked him unconscious before he could see it was me."

He paused and looked at me, "I did not kill him. You can see he is standing right here. I wanted the vineyard manager's job.

"I have done nothing wrong! I did not kidnap anyone. I was just trying to collect the reward money. I did not kill anyone. I was just trying to protect myself and the winery. I have no idea where Bea is!"

"Jose'," began Sheriff Longo, "You almost killed Trevor. You planted evidence in the vineyard implicating Hector. Those are serious criminal offenses. It is called Tampering with or Fabricating Physical Evidence and it is a third-degree felony punishable for two to twenty years in prison.

"Assaulting Trevor with the grape vine trunk is aggravated assault with a deadly weapon and is a second-degree felony punishable by two to twenty years in prison.

"Are you getting the message here? You will be going to jail for a long time so before it gets worse, where is Bea?"

"I do not know where Bea is! I told you that already."

Sheriff Longo read him his rights and took him to jail. "This time you are an adult, José, and will be spending time in a real jail not juvenile detention."

Chapter 17

I called Danny to let him know that we found Oto's killer. It was Héctor. Danny did not sound surprised, "I felt it must have been someone who knew Oto."

I learned later that after Danny thanked me and hung up, he at once called Bea, *"Héctor was the killer,"* he told her. *"It is safe for you to come home now. Héctor is in custody.*

"The Sheriff was looking for you. He insisted there is no way you could have had anything to do with Oto's murder. I knew he and the vineyard investigator would question me. That is why I did not want to know where you were."

Bea was shocked that Héctor was the killer. She said, "Why?"

Danny told her, "I do not know why but maybe the Sheriff and Trevor know."

After I hung up from Danny, I told Sheriff Longo that I was going to Bea's house to see if I could find any clues as to where she might be. The door was open, so I walked into the kitchen. I thought to myself, "Kristy must have left the door open."

On the table was a pad and pencil. The top page had been removed. The second page had impressions from the first sheet. I carefully rubbed the impression with pencil lead revealing what was written on the second page.

It said, 'Red River Inn'. I jumped in my car and headed toward the Red River Inn which is near the Oklahoma border with Texas.

As I drove along Highway 377, I stopped at businesses along the way to see if they had seen an attractive lady matching the description of Bea. I showed them a photo of me with Bea that I took in the vineyard when I first met Oto and Bea. No one had seen her.

When I got to Sherman, I stopped at the Sherman Hills Winery and talked to Bobbie Sherman. Bobbie and Bea were old friends. They served on the Board of North Texas Grape Growers together. Bobbie told me she had not seen Oto or Bea for at least two years, ever since both of them went off the board.

I continued north until I reached the Red River Inn. When I arrived, I showed the front desk clerk Bea's photo. He told me she had checked in a few days ago and that he had seen her car leave early that morning, but he did not recall her checking out.

Bea drove a yellow Mercedes 350E so I went into Denison to see if I could find her. Bea had told me once that she loved history so I headed to the Grayson County Frontier Village. The village includes the birthplace of US President Dwight Eisenhower. I thought she might have checked out his house, but why would she be touring the countryside if she thought everyone was looking for her? She was not there.

Denison was also the home of horticulturalist T.V. Munson who is credited with saving the French wine industry by creating phylloxera-resistant vines. His contribution was so significant that he was inducted into the French Legion of Honor. I thought she might have looked for his experimental vineyard. She was not there but a docent at the museum suggested I check the Denison Wine Bar.

Parked outside the wine bar was her yellow car. Inside the wine bar, Bea was sitting alone in a corner with her back to the wall. She appeared to be afraid of being seen.

"Bea?" I asked as I approached her. She looked at me cautiously and said, "yes."

"Do you remember me? Trevor Talan with Texas A&M University?"

"Oh yes, hi Trevor. Please join me."

"Are you OK?" I asked. "Kristy is worried about you."

"I am so sorry for leaving so quickly. I was afraid when I heard Oto had been killed," she cried. "I did not know what to do."

"I understand, Bea. Hector has confessed to killing Oto."

"I know," Bea said, "Danny told me. When Oto was killed, Danny told me to leave town until Oto's killer was found. He was afraid Oto's killer would be after me. Danny did not even know where I was."

I followed her back to Red River Inn where she gathered her things and then followed her back to her home in Argyle.

"Thank you so much, Trevor. I appreciate your help. Would you like to come in for a glass of wine? I have so many questions."

"I know you do, and I am happy to answer what I do know."

"Trevor, why would Héctor do this? Where is he being held?"

"Héctor is in custody with Sheriff Longo at the county jail. He did tell me during his confession that Oto had promised him part of the vineyard in your will but that Oto had betrayed him by writing a new will and giving everything to Kristy.

"Héctor was very bitter, Bea. He was no longer in charge. His wife left him for a lover in California. She depleted his savings with all of her gambling. Finally, the last straw was hearing that he was out of the will."

Bea began to weep. Kristy walked in.

"Mom, Mom, are you ok? Where have you been? What is wrong?" she asked as she gave her mom a hug.

Bea and I explained all that had happened. Kristy looked so sad and lamented. "I am so sorry, Mom. You and Dad worked so hard. You were just trying to help me preserve the winery.

"I am flabbergasted about Héctor. You helped Héctor's wife when she went in the hospital for an emergency appendectomy. You even cooked dinner for Héctor until Stella was able to return to full duties. How ungrateful!"

Kristy excitedly changed the subject, "Mom, you would be so proud of me and Trevor. We thought you were kidnapped. I received a call from a muffle-voiced man who demanded $50,000. He said he had kidnapped you and was holding you ransom. I raised the $50,000 and awaited his call. He called the second time and I demanded to speak to you. He panicked and hung up."

Kristy began talking faster and faster, relaying her story. "When Héctor was arrested, the sheriff asked him if he suspected anyone of kidnapping you. Héctor said José had been bragging that he was coming into a lot of money.

"Then the sheriff and Trevor went to Josés house and found the phone that José used to call me. That seemed very suspicious. After they asked José where he was going to get all that money, he confessed. Then, they discovered that José had been in juvenile detention as a teen for stealing money from a church."

Kristy took a deep breath and told her mom, "I am so happy you were never kidnapped and that you are okay."

Bea looked at Kristy and took her hand. "Thank you so much for working so hard to help me. I love you. Where did you get the money for the ransom?"

Kristy admitted, "I took it out of my teacher savings, Mom. The winery still has money problems."

Bea got teary eyed and said, "I am so thankful that we now know the true heart of Héctor and his troubled life. He stole your father from you and the love of my life from me. I do not want this to cast a shadow on your relationship with Mathew or your upcoming marriage."

"Thank you, Mom, I can't believe Dad is gone. He was so excited about Mathew and about giving me away. Who will give me away now?"

Bea looked at me and then at Kristy, "What about the person who found your father's murderer, Trevor? Trevor has taken such good care of us and he will be collaborating with you to transition the vineyard."

Kristy looked at me, "Do you mind, Trevor? I believe my dad would like you filling in for him and I would love to have you be part of our wedding."

"It would be my pleasure and a wonderful way to honor your dad. Plus, it will give me experience so when I ask Lulu to marry me, I will do it right." I replied.

Kristy excitedly probed, "Oh my goodness, Trevor, when are you going to pop the question?"

"Very soon. Please don't share this with her."

Kristy smiled, "I would never steal her surprise. I know Lulu loves you very much, and she has agreed to be my Maid of Honor. She will be ready when you ask.

"She even told me confidentially that she was surprised you had not popped the question already. She was afraid you had cold feet."

I smiled and nodded thoughtfully, "I have wanted to ask her at just the right time and place. I have loved her from the first time I met her. She brightens up my life."

Chapter 18

I looked at Bea and Kristy and shared that I had some possible great news to help with winery finances. They both looked at me hopefully.

"SUSTA, the Southern United States Trade Association, have grants available to wineries that wish to expand distribution into South America. That could be a salvation for the winery."

"Thank you, Trevor, that is wonderful news", encouraged Bea. "Arrgos Cellars is the largest producer of Tempranillo in Texas and that grape is in very high demand in South America. It could open up a new market and the grant money could help pay off the debt."

Kristy solicited, "Can you please tell me more about the SUSTA program?"

I pulled up the details on my phone. "SUSTA is one of four non-profit trade groups that help United States companies build their global business. They will teach you how to export and they will find appropriate markets for your products.

"Spanish wines sell very well in South America. As you know, Tempranillo is the principle grape in the Spanish wines.

"The SUSTA programs provide you with up to fifty percent reimbursement for generation of new sales in South America. SUSTA resources are well placed in the market and can give you distributors, key retailers, and restaurant chains to get your Tempranillo into the marketplace. This will give you a global reputation that will probably help you in your American market.

"I am happy to help you fill out the paperwork."

Kristy thanked me and responded, "Let's wait until after the wedding. Then I will have more time to focus on it. It does take an extra burden off my shoulders to know there may be a way out of our debt. Thank you so much, Trevor.

"How could life be better? Mathew and I are marrying at the winery. Mom and Lulu are helping me with the details."

A few days later Bea showed up at the winery with a briefcase. "Hi Mom, thank you so much for coming to help me."

Bea and Kristy hugged. Bea set her briefcase down and said, "I brought a copy of our "Wedding Planner". Let's fill it out together and see what we need to do."

Kristy was excited to get started, "Wonderful! I brought magazines and photos of what I want. I have had a wedding file in my room since I was little girl. In it are articles and photos of what my dream wedding would be. Look at this article about what to do first."

Bea suggests, "The first thing we must do is set a budget. Unfortunately, we do not have a lot of money to spend. Let's be creative and design something using the assets that we have.

"Maybe we could ask some of our suppliers if they would like to sponsor elements of the wedding. We spend a lot of money on vineyard equipment, bottles, corks, and production chemicals. They can help us."

With that in mind, they walked the property and chose a peninsula near the winery lake for the ceremony. "Look, Mom, it already has a gazebo covered with pink Peggy Martin roses and the green grassy lawn looks ready for white folding chairs. It could be beautiful."

"Pink and green are your favorite colors so let's plan around that," said Bea, "I will schedule a meeting for you with Monie Smith. I spoke with her over the phone and she is happy to help us. I have worked with her on other weddings and she is very talented."

Kristy responded, "I love pink hydrangeas! Can she get those? Did you know that they symbolize love and emotion? They even say that the flower resembles a beating heart.

"And I would like for her to incorporate rosemary sprigs in remembrance of Dad, lavender because it symbolizes serenity, grace, and calmness. There has been so much turmoil in our lives recently."

Bea added, "Kristy, you also like stargazer lilies because they are so wonderfully fragrant, and white looks beautiful against your alabaster skin. Let's also include those."

Kristy nodded, "I love these ideas. And what do you think we should do for the groomsmen? Mathew loves yellow tulips. Do you think we could incorporate those?"

Bea smiled, "I think Monie can get whatever flowers and herbs you want. I like that yellow tulips stand for cheerful thoughts and sunshine because that is my hope and desire for you and Mathew's future. You could even add a yellow tulip in the other florals as well to tie them all together. Monie has been doing this for many years. She will be able to do it beautifully."

Kristy was getting excited, "Now can we talk about the guest list? I understand we need to keep it small.

"We could invite our new distributor and his family. We should invite our new winemaker and his family along with our staff. Sheriff Longo's family is a must. Danny, our District Attorney, and his family. Our family and Mathew's family. We should also invite Amit Dhingra, Trevor's boss at Texas A&M University.

"Oh, and we must invite Lulu's orphanage family since she will be my maid of honor.

"What about the Governor of Texas? He was such a good friend of Dad. The Governor was our State Senator. You and Dad chaired his election committee. When he ran for governor you raised a lot of money for his campaign. He even appointed Dad to his Agricultural Advisory Committee. I know he would love to be invited.

As Kristy and Bea talked, the guest list continued to grow.

"This is exhausting!" exclaimed Kristy, "Getting married is much more difficult than I thought. There are so many considerations."

Bea hugged Kristy and said, "May God grant that you will only do this once in your life. It will be the largest and best party you should ever host, so savor every moment and be joyful."

Chapter 19

There was a beautiful sunrise on the day of the wedding. The date was March 21st. The vines were turning green. It was the hallelujah period in the vineyard.

That is when the new branches emerge from the cordon arms and they reach straight up to the heavens. I remembered Bea comparing us to branches. In John 15 of the Bible, the Lord says, *"I am the vine, you are the branches. If you remain in Me and I in you, you will produce much fruit."*

The fruit clusters were formed and beginning to debut the future vintage. It was a beautiful symbol of the joy of new life together for Mr. and Mrs. Mathew Koreni. It did not elude me that Mathew's last name Koreni meant "roots" in Serbian.

Roots are the most important part of the vine. Healthy roots in healthy soil create the best plants with the best chance to have long life and produce good fruit. I pray that will be the case as the Koreni's build their new life together and rebuild the life of the winery.

Sheriff Longo was all dressed up in his official Sheriff's uniform. He even wore his new Sheriff's hat. Danny was dressed in his black tuxedo, as was Mathew. Kristy's Maid of Honor was Lulu, who had become very close to Kristy. She looked gorgeous in a pink off-the-shoulder chiffon gown. I had never seen her look so beautiful.

The Fabulous Brookwoods supplied the music. The Brookwoods met Oto and Bea in 2004 when they were the featured band on a Royal Caribbean Cruise to Cozumel. The lead singer and his wife founded Messina Hof Wine Cellars. They have passed it to their son and daughter-in-law just as Oto and Bea have passed Arrgos Cellars to Kristy.

The Brookwoods started playing the song "Feelings" and the attendees became quiet. All were excited to see how beautiful Kristy looked.

Sweat was running down Sheriff Longo's brow which was no surprise since this was the first wedding he was to perform. He received his ordination from the Universal Church in California just two weeks ago.

He was so proud of his official documentation. He even got it framed and brought his certificate with him to show me. He had asked me if he should get the official robes that came with the certificate but I told him that he looked handsome and official in his sheriff's uniform.

I was standing on luxurious forest green grass near the gazebo which was draped in vibrant pink roses. Their fragrance filled the air. The vineyard was to my left and the lake to my right.

Visions of me nervously proposing to Lulu for her hand in marriage filled my head. She has become my partner for life. As soon as I awake, I think of her. She has such a deep spiritual soul. I, on the other hand, was a cultural Christian, but I did not bring the Lord into my daily life.

I grew up to be a fixer. A fixer believes more in themselves than their belief in the Lord. Since Lulu has come into my life, the Lord is now my fixer and I remain dependent upon His guidance. That direction serves me well. I no longer worry. Lulu and I grow closer in our faith and I have never been happier.

So, on this glorious day, I hope Lulu's and my happiness are shared by all those that are attending, and, most of all Kristy, Mathew, and Bea. Lulu's favorite song was also "Feelings" so my thoughts were of her as I awaited Kristy.

Standing there next to Mathew and Sheriff Longo I reflected on how we have become so close. I admire Mathew's love and devotion for Kristy and the dedication to duty of Sheriff Longo. I smiled at the sheriff and he smiled back. He no longer seemed nervous.

Mathew, on the other hand, was as nervous as a Serbian farmer who was "shaking like a Serbian Sunflower". I hugged him and said, "The Lord is with you, and He is here to bless your union with Kristy." Mathew stopped shaking.

I returned to the back of the ceremony to await Kristy's arrival.

Bea seemed so happy. Her sadness of Oto's death had now become replaced by Kristy's joy and happiness.

Kristy surprised everyone when she showed up on the vineyard tractor decorated with yellow tulip-adorned grapevine wreaths that Kristy had made and decorated herself. I was even surprised. I thought she would be driven to the ceremony by someone else.

She wanted to show that she was in charge and that the winery was in competent hands. Glowing and radiant, she stopped the tractor and I helped her off.

All of the problems she had faced these past months seemed to vanish. I saw a confident and joyful Kristy. She was the new Arrgos Cellars CEO, about to be married to the love of her life, Mathew. When she heard the song "Feelings," her eyes teared up. I gave her my handkerchief and she said, "I am so ready. Let's do this."

As we walked down the aisle, she confidently acknowledged her family and friends with a broad smile.

As we approached Sheriff Longo and Mathew, we could see they both had tears of joy on their cheeks. I handed Kristy over to Mathew and said, "God bless you both. May your walk together with the Lord bring you a long and prosperous marriage."

Mathew took Kristy's hand and looked into her eyes with great adoration. The two of them faced Sheriff Longo who said, "The two of you have prepared your vows. Kristy, please recite yours first."

Kristy said, "Mathew, you have come into my life at a very difficult time. You have brought me joy, stability, and tranquility. Your wisdom has helped me, guided me, and strengthened me. I look forward to being your wife so that I can bring you joy and happiness for all the days of our lives and beyond.

"You are my best friend and the man I love deeply. I pledge to you my undying love and devotion. I will honor you and obey you all the days of my life. As we grow old together I will always be there for you. I am honored to be beside you as your wife."

Sheriff Longo said, "Mathew, what is your vow?"

"Kristy, you are the sexiest woman I know. You are my inspiration in life. You are joy when there is sorrow. You are hope when there is despair. You are my soulmate. I love your tender heart and beautiful soul. I will honor you and be faithful to you all of my life. I will stand by your side in any of life's challenges.

"At night, when we go to bed I will hug you, caress you, and tell you each and every night that I am a lucky man. I love you deeply and I am honored to be beside you as your husband. In these past few months, I have seen a woman who has blossomed in the face of despair. You are a fragrant flower and a warm and caring person. I will always cherish you. I look forward to growing old with you."

It felt as though a wave of love rolled from the congregation to the altar embracing the two as they looked at each other.

Sheriff Longo said, "I have a few words to say. I have known Kristy since she was a baby. I am her godfather. She is a devoted Christian and selfless teacher. I was proud yet fearful when she took the job of teaching in an inner-city school in New York. As she grew up she developed such inner strength and that inner strength has helped her to get her through these troubled times.

"Her perseverance will give her the ability to adapt to new challenges. I have always been and will always be so proud of her. She will make an effective leader of Arrgos Cellars and a wonderful wife to Mathew. I am proud to officiate this wedding, and Mathew, you are a very, very lucky man.

"On the other hand, I have known Mathew for a much shorter period of time. He appears to be an honorable, honest, and caring man. I have seen him in the courtroom. He is a great student of the law and a tenacious attorney. I have seen great compassion toward his clients, and he has a wonderful reputation in Dallas as well as this community. I know that if Kristy believes in him, he is a good man. Kristy, I know that he will never let you down.

"Well, ladies and gentlemen, if there is no one here who objects to this marriage, I now pronounce Mathew and Kristy, Mr. and Mrs. Mathew Koreni. Congratulations to the bride and groom."

The crowd all cheered.

The happy couple danced down the aisle to their waiting car to be whisked away to their honeymoon in Albania and Serbia where they could trace their family roots and heritages. They spent a week in each country. They met many members of their families. Bea looked after the winery during their trip.

Chapter 20

Upon their return, Bea had planned a surprise welcome party for them with family and friends. She had the front door decorated in pink and green with pots of yellow tulips and pink hydrangeas lining the sidewalk.

Kristy and Mathew gave hugs all around and eagerly shared what they had experienced on their honeymoon.

Showing photos of their trip, Kristy started, "Albania is a land of stunning landscapes. The Albania riviera had incredible beaches. The rugged Albanian alps were filled with lakes and rivers. We saw so many archeological sites, castles, ancient cities, and two incredible UNESCO heritage sites. The culture is so diverse with roots from Greek, Roman, Byzantine, and Ottoman occupation. I was amazed to see Muslims, Christians, and Bektashi all living in harmony.

"The authentic Albanian cuisine is delicious. I have always loved Mom's Byrek savory pastry and Tavekosi, the incredible baked lamb with yogurt. To taste these in their land of origin was so special. I even brought back their recipes.

"My absolute favorite was their outstanding seafood. I do have to admit that the Albanian language, Shqiptar, was very challenging. It reminded me of hearing Mom and Dad speak when they did not want me to understand what they were saying."

Byrek Recipe

Ingredients

For the dough:
- *4 cups all-purpose flour*
- *1 ½ cups warm water*
- *1 teaspoon salt*
- *2 tablespoons olive oil*
  (Or purchase Phyllo Dough)

For the filling:
- *1-pound fresh spinach, washed and chopped*
- *1 cup crumbled feta cheese*
- *1 large onion, finely chopped*
- *2 tablespoons olive oil*
- *¼ cup white wine (Messina Hof Gewurztraminer)*
- *Salt and pepper to taste*
- *1 egg*
- *Paprika for dusting*

Instructions:

1. *Prepare the dough. In a large mixing bowl, combine the flour and salt. Gradually add warm water, mixing until a soft dough forms.*

2. *Knead the dough on a floured surface for about 10 minutes until smooth and elastic. Divide the dough into small balls (about 8-10 pieces), cover with a damp cloth, and let rest for at least 30 minutes.*

3. *Prepare the filling. In a large, lidded pan, heat the olive oil over medium heat. Add the chopped onion and sauté until soft and translucent. Add wine and cook until reduced by half. Add the spinach and cook until wilted. Season with salt and pepper. Remove from heat and let cool slightly.*

4. *Mix in the crumbled feta cheese and beaten egg.*

5. *Preheat the oven to 375 degrees F. On a floured surface, roll out each dough ball into a very thin sheet, as thin as possible without tearing. Brush each sheet with olive oil, lightly dust with paprika, and layer them, one on top of the other, in a large baking dish, allowing the edges to hang over the sides. Save one sheet for the topping.*

6. *Spread the spinach and feta filling evenly over the layered dough. Fold the overhanging dough over the filling, and place another rolled out sheet on top, tucking the edges inside.*

7. *Brush the top with olive oil.*

8. *Bake in a preheated oven for 30-40 minutes or until the top is golden brown and crispy. Let cool slightly before cutting into squares or slices and service.*

Tave Kosi Recipe

Ingredients
- *4 tablespoons butter*
- *1 tablespoon olive oil*
- *3-pound boneless lamb shoulder, cut into 2-inch cubes*
- *4 cloves garlic, grated*
- *1 teaspoon dried oregano*
- *¼ cup water*
- *¼ cup Messina Hof Merlot*

- *1/3 cup long-grain rice, rinsed in cold water*
- *½ cup all-purpose flour*
- *15 ounces Greek style yogurt*
- *5 ounces sour cream*
- *5 eggs, beaten*
- *Freshly grated nutmeg*
- *Salt and black pepper*

Preparation

1. *Preheat oven to 350F.*

2. *Heat half of the butter and the olive oil in a large, lidded pan over a high heat. Brown the lamb in batches.*

3. *Return all the lamb to the pan. Add the garlic, oregano and 1/4 cup of water and wine. Bring to a simmer and cook, covered with a lid, for about 45-50 minutes until the lamb is tender.*

4. *Stir in the rice and season with salt and pepper. Transfer to a 3-quart ovenproof dish.*

5. *Melt the remaining butter in a small saucepan, add the flour and make a roux, cook for 2 minutes, then take off the heat. Add the yogurt and sour cream and mix well. Then return to the heat and cook gently for a couple of minutes. Take off the heat, add the beaten eggs and season with salt and pepper.*

6. *Pour the sauce over the lamb and rice mixture, grate fresh nutmeg on top and put back in the oven for 40-45 minutes until starting to turn golden-brown.*

7. *Remove from the oven and allow to sit for 5 minutes before serving.*

Kristy turned to Mathew and said, "What were your special moments in Serbia?"

Mathew smiled and playfully answered, "Just being with you was like being in heaven."

Kristy blushed and nudging him said, "No, tell them what you found fascinating about Serbia."

Mathew nodded and continued, "First, I was surprised how similar the historical background of Serbia was to Albania. Serbia, too, had Roman, Byzantine, and Ottoman heritages, but they also had Austro-Hungarian in their background. Serbia is a country of eastern and western influences.

"My favorite Serbian food was cevapi which is grilled meats. I also liked Sarma which are stuffed cabbage rolls. I loved putting Ajvar on my meat. It is a peppery based condiment.

"The fertile plain of Bojbodina rising up to the mountains of the Dinaric Alps and Carpathian Mountains were breathtaking. I was so happy that we were there for the Serbian World Music Festival."

Kristy chimed in that she loved finding the Banitsa pastry at the Nicola Tesla Pastry shop in Belgrade.

As I was leaving the party, I reminded Kristy, "Remember that Phillip Moore, the wine consultant, will be spending three days with you to develop wine protocols, to taste and blend with you so that your wines will regain the reputation they once had."

In the depths of tragedy, we find the strength to rebuild and the hope for a brighter tomorrow.

The next day, Philip Moore arrived at the winery. Kristy invited him to the lab where she had already prepared samples of all the wine lots. She was kind enough to ask me to join them.

Philip tasted through all the wines and then said, "Well Kristy, are you ready to hear what I think?"

With trepidation, Kristy said, "Let me have it. What do you think?"

"I think your big red wines like Tempranillo, Cabernet Sauvignon, and Merlot could use a little more color. I see that you make Petit Verdot and Petit Sirah, so I would recommend adding five percent of either of them into the blend. The wines will have better color and look more appealing in the glass.

"I think the wines are a little bit too tannic. Oto was probably leaving the wine on the skins a little too long. By reducing the tannin, you can make the wines sing and become yummier.

"You could accomplish this by adding five percent of Petit Sirah to one blend and five percent of Petit Verdot to another blend. After you do the trial bench blends, we can taste both for color and balance.

"The white wines like Pinot Grigio, Sauvignon Blanc, and Trebbiano do not have enough acidity. I would recommend adjusting the ph shortly after the grapes are pressed to make the wines crisper and more exciting to the palate. You could even hedge the Sauvignon Blanc vines to give it more gooseberry character.

"Oto really knew how to make port. They have an exquisite chocolate cherry flavor. To think he was able to make nineteen percent alcohol without adding brandy is amazing.

"I see that he uses K1 yeast which can ferment up to nineteen percent alcohol if you re-inoculate with the K1 every seven days for four weeks."

Oto utilized sequential inoculation developed by Paul V Bonarrigo at Messina Hof Winery in 1986. He kept the yeast active by sequentially adding the yeast until the alcohol reached 19% without adding brandy.

My recommendation of Philip Moore as the wine consultant has paid off. This year Philip and Kristy's collaboration has resulted in a saddle at the Houston Livestock Show and Rodeo, Best in Show for the Reserve Tempranillo. The wines have become dark, rich, and very full-bodied. They resemble the best of Spain with the lush fruit character typical of Texas sun, and boy are they 'yummy'!

Kristy reached out to me to let me know that wine sales in South America were going very well. She hired Héctor's replacement, a vineyard manager from Michigan, and many positive changes have been made to the vineyard program.

Arrgos Cellars has expanded by establishing wineries outside of San Antonio, outside of Austin, and outside of Houston. Their wines are featured in many of the top ten restaurants in Texas. Oto would be proud. Bea now lives in Grapevine and has become very active in the Wine Pouring Society. She visits Argyle often. Kristy says Bea keeps asking about a grandbaby.

Recently we all got invited to an anniversary party at Mathew and Kristy's new home. When Lulu and I got there, Bea was already helping in the kitchen. The house was modernly decorated in whites and grays. The living room was uniquely designed with a ceiling of what looked like puffy white clouds. I had never seen anything like it.

Lulu whispered, "Are those the real ceiling or is it decoration? Look, Trevor, clouds!"

I shrugged my shoulders and hoped Lulu would not want a ceiling like that.

Kristy and Mathew looked very much in love. They called everyone together into the living room for a toast.

Mathew invited all of us to raise our glasses and spoke, "To all of you who have stood by us, supported us, and encouraged us through our journey, Kristy and I thank you from the bottom of our hearts. Oto is also here with us in spirit.

"We know it was the Lord who brought us all together in this life and it is from Him all our blessings fall."

With that he and Kristy reached up and pulled on an invisible string that looked like fishing line. Suddenly, out of the clouds blue confetti, blue curling ribbons and blue pacifiers fell.

Bea squealed, "Are you having a baby?!"

Kristy beamed and said, "Mathew and I are expecting. We just had an ultrasound. It is a baby boy."

Everyone began to clap. Mathew gave Kristy a hug and a kiss. Then he added, "In honor of Kristy's father, we will name our baby boy, Oto."

Bea teared up and raised her glass, "When you believe in the Lord, 'Everything is truly possible.'"

Oto's death was tragic but out of tragedy comes blessings and rejoicing.

List of Characters

Trevor Talan – Doctor of Viticulture and investigator, narrator of the story

Oto Arrgos – Founder of the winery, Arrgos Cellars, husband of Bea and father of Kristy

Bea Arrgos – Founder of the winery, Arrgos Cellars, wife of Oto and mother of Kristy.

Kristy Arrgos– the Arrgos daughter, fiancé of Mathew Koreni

Sheriff Longo – Local law enforcement

Héctor – Arrgos Vineyard Manager

José – Arrgos Vineyard Assistant Manager

Phillip Moore – Winemaker Consultant

Lulu – Girlfriend of Trevor Talan

Mathew Koreni – Attorney born in Serbia, engaged to Kristy. Serbian name for Mathew is Mateja.

Stella – Héctor's wife

Danny – District attorney and attorney for Arrgos Cellars

Sal – Kristy's high school boyfriend

About the Authors

Paul V. and Merrill Bonarrigo founded Messina Hof Vineyard in 1977 in Bryan, Texas, as pioneers of the Texas grape and wine industries. Today, Messina Hof has four wineries around Texas and continues to be one of the most awarded wineries in Texas in regional, national, and international competitions. The Messina Hof legacy continues with their son, Paul M, and his wife, Karen.

Paul V. Bonarrigo, born in the shadow of Yankee Stadium and graduated from Columbia University, served in the Navy during Vietnam, and studied winemaking at the University of California–Davis while stationed in California. Merrill Bonarrigo, a native of Bryan–College Station, Texas, graduated from Texas A&M University with a degree in business management and taught Wine Retailing at University of Houston.

Paul and Merrill introduced Sagrantino grapes to Texas. They have traveled to thirty-eight countries to teach wine hospitality and successful generational transition. They lead wine tour groups around the world, blog, and author books:

Ultimate Food and Wine Pairing Cookbook

Ultimate Food and Wine Pairing Cookbook II

Vineyard Cuisine, Meals, and Memories from Messina Hof

Family, Tradition and Romance—The Messina Hof Story

Curse of Estacado—The Trail of Blood and Wine

Blood on the Brazos – The Trail of Blood and Wine

Death on the Pedernales – The Trail of Blood and Wine

www.ingramcontent.com/pod-product-compliance
Lightning Source LLC
Chambersburg PA
CBHW070502170726
48291CB00008B/2619